She paused and narrowed her eyes at him, maybe a little regretful for coming on so strong to a new neighbor. "Look, I've been up all night and I may be a little irritable. All I ask is that you keep it quiet, okay?"

She was damn near as tall as he was, and he stared almost directly into those large brown eyes, smiling like a kid on Christmas morning. "Why don't you come in and let me cook you breakfast? I think I've got an egg somewhere."

The tightness in her jaw softened a bit. "And if you don't, you'll lay one, right?"

Wild thoughts of being raped by a mad neighbor lady rushed through Larry's mind. "Come on, what do you have to lose?"

(Cover Photograph Posed By Professional Model)

Moving Up

Ron Montana

TOWER BOOKS NEW YORK CITY

This novel is dedicated to Robyn North
who is okay in anybody's book

A TOWER BOOK

Published by

Tower Publications, Inc.
Two Park Avenue
New York, N.Y. 10016

PART ONE

Larry, Robyn, Lynn and Flash

ONE

Fighting for peace is like fucking for virginity. No draft.
These words were spray-painted in silver drippings across
the back wall of the high-school gymnasium in foot-high
letters. Larry DiaMonte frowned and shook his head as he
drove past it, steering the red Turbo Porsche onto the
basketball courts that fronted the soccer field.

The graffiti irritated him, maybe more than it would
have a few months ago. He had a lot to be irritated with
lately. It was a lousy day in mid-October. There was a first-
stage smog alert over the valley, the worst in five years,
and it was hot. It was that clinging, miserable heat that
oppressed the Los Angeles basin, when the sky grayed up
so badly you could only see the outline of the Universal
tower from the Hollywood freeway.

He had left the icy air conditioning of his car to venture
into the furnace outside twice today, once from his town
house in Granada Hills to his office in Studio City and now
to his son's soccer game. A light breeze that offered no
relief blew dust clouds over the dirt field. He looked for a
place to park away from the swirling grit. He had just
washed the damn car this morning and it would be nice if
he could keep it clean for a day or so.

Parking in the shade next to the corner wall of the gym,

he got out and locked the car, leaning over to chip at a spot of tree sap on the hood with his fingernail, wondering how he had missed that one. He straightened up and raised his sunglasses to his forehead, squinting at the bleachers that lined one side of the field. He was early, the kids were just lining up to do their calisthenics. Rubbing at his short, neatly trimmed black beard, he walked to the front of the car and flicked away a piece of cotton from the washing mitt that had gotten caught in the license plate holder. He looked at the plate and sighed. The yellow letters read: AH MUSE. He tightened the muscles in his jaw and began the long walk to the bleachers.

He didn't recognize his son until the lanky fifteen-year-old waved to him from the line. They all looked alike in the tight blue shorts and orange shirts. Like spindly-legged mantises with terminal acne, he thought. "Hey, Dad! What'd the cop say today?" Steve gave him a toothy grin and Larry almost believed he was glad to see him again. He smiled back at the boy's reference to his driving habits and it almost seemed like old times as he threw the kid the thumbs-up sign.

Larry was a man of medium height and a dark complexion that bespoke his Sicilian ancestry. He ran a hand through his semicurly hair and looked at his mirror image in Steve. The boy was almost as tall as he was, and would probably be taller. It's funny when you don't see them for a few weeks how much older they look, he thought, as he noticed Steve had put on some weight. Soon he would be approaching Larry's lean 165, and if he decided to grow a beard it would be difficult to tell father and son apart.

"Your mother coming today?" He kept smiling, for Steve's sake, but the hollow feeling that contracted his gut every time he thought of Robyn came back stronger than ever.

"Yeah, she said she was, if she don't have an appointment. You know how that goes."

I sure do, Larry said silently to himself. He nodded and moved toward the bleachers. Taking a seat on the rough wood plank, he glanced around at the half-dozen other parents that had come to watch the game. There was nobody he was on more than a hello basis with, and that was good. He sure the hell didn't feel like any conversation right now.

Larry DiMonte sat back and looked at the brown sky. He had turned forty last November. He recalled his birthday, which had fallen on Thanksgiving day, and the knot in his stomach got tighter. It was almost his birthday again and he had been separated from his wife of sixteen years for exactly four months and eighteen days.

Sixteen years! Jesus, she even had him thinking it was sixteen years. She had been six months pregnant when they got married. Ergo the extra year. She had always wondered if that was the reason he had married her. He had always said no, that he was a free spirit, and that something like a kid on the way wouldn't have prevented him from doing exactly what he wanted.

Now he wasn't so sure. What if he hadn't married her? He looked at Steve toeing a practice ball in between a teammate's legs. She would have gotten an abortion. He knew that as sure as he knew he'd be a year older in less than a month. He looked up at the hazy sun. God, give me the strength, give me the strength to strangle her with my bare hands if she shows up. Oh—and Lord? Make it look like an accident, okay?

Hey, not a bad idea for a script. Guy murders his wife and makes it look so much like an act of God that nobody suspects him. Then he gets conscience stricken and confesses, but the cops won't buy it. Shit, sounds like a rerun of *Columbo,* Larry, better stick to what you do best.

He removed a cigarette from his shirt pocket. He was

trying to keep them at least an hour apart, but he was failing miserably. Maybe he should have stayed with the pipe he'd smoked for ten years, but the damned tobacco had gotten all over everything. Robyn had complained about that daily. He made a mental note to go out and buy a new meerschaum tomorrow.

So what if it had been an old *Columbo* episode? Maybe he could work the idea into a three-part *Two Families*. He inhaled deeply and blew the smoke at the sun. Christ, the numbers on the series opener had been phenomenal! A 27.7 rating and a 43 share. That, sweetheart, meant a 55 to 60 million viewer tune-in every Monday night at nine. The outlandish sitcom about a divorced couple who live in opposite sides of the same duplex with their new spouses and children had blown away the opposition like a Kansas tornado.

Until the last couple of weeks, that is. The other two networks and their fucking counterprogramming had knocked them from first to eighth place, according to last Thursday's Nielsens. Who knew people would watch a special dealing with the marriage of a pig sex symbol and a frog? Or that ABC would run *Star Trek, the Motion Picture* on Sunday night and let it spill over to Monday?

Who knew? God knew, that's who, and He had obviously singled out the executive story editor of *Two Families Too Many* because he hadn't seen the inside of a church since his son's confirmation.

Larry's show had been called the "million dollar a week" series after the first three episodes. And for good reason. *Two Families* commanded from advertisers $165,000 for each thirty-second-commercial spot during the program. That meant the network gross was just under a million a week. That rate was based upon the number of viewers reached, and no series coud bring in higher revenue as long as it maintained its rating lead. It was

Larry's job to see that it did. He had good reason to bitch about divine intervention.

Steve's team lined up facing the opposing players in the center of the field, while the referee checked their shoes. Larry looked back at the parking area. Maybe she wasn't going to show at all. His thoughts wandered back to BarRon Productions, where he directed two story editors and a bevy of writers. Before joining BarRon, he had written for *All In the Family, M.A.S.H.* and *Welcome Back, Kotter* sporadically. *Two Families* had been his brainchild and he had sold it to BarRon, and then to the network himself. Even when the network issued a thumbs down to the original concept and ordered another pilot, he had not been deterred. He knew it would be a hit, and he kept the faith. But it sure the hell was a lot of work. He needed three stories a week, main theme, sub plot, and runner. All made more difficult because *Two Families* was not just a sitcom or a straight drama, but hopefully a successful blending of the two.

Every script considered had to be rewritten by him and his two crazy coworkers, Patte Gordon and Lew Beckerman, not because of poor writing, but to conform to the octopus that consisted of budget, network standards and practices, and cast changes, to name a few of the myriad daily hurdles. But that was just the tip of the iceberg. Larry had to do a constant rewriting job up to the tapings, and sometimes well into them. It was a ballbreaking occupation, and the upheaval in his personal life was not helping matters any.

They seemed to always be behind two weeks for every one they advanced, barely keeping one step ahead of the tapings, and Larry was bone tired most of the time.

Turning his head again, he looked to the entrance of the field beyond the basketball courts. His neck was beginning to ache when he craned it to see if every car pulling

11

in was Robyn's forest-green Seville. This time, the bright grille work of the Caddy glared back at him, and his armpits and the palms of his hands were suddenly damp. His throat felt like he had just swallowed a mouthful of sand. He could hear his heartbeat pounding in his ears.

He tried to calm himself as he watched her slot the car next to his Porsche and get out. She walked the hundred or so yards to the bleachers with Lawrence Jr. running ahead with the exuberance only a nine-year-old could attain. Larry pretended to watch the field as the referee gave instructions to the two teams. Robyn stopped to speak to another mother who sat in a folding chair near the end line, which gave Larry the opportunity to study her.

She was five foot one and weighed one hundred and five pounds, and damn, she looked beautiful. She was wearing a three-piece summer suit in muted browns, and the reddish highlights in her long blonde hair danced around her head like a halo. He looked at the curve of her breasts straining against the silk blouse as she leaned down with her arm on the back of the chair. 34-C. He still had the beat-up size chart she had given him when they were married. It was barely readable, but he had it memorized. Funny thing, it didn't really matter; she never changed, except during the two pregnancies, and even then it had taken her only a few weeks to get back to a size seven.

She laughed at something the other woman said and his heart sank. How the hell could she be so damn happy when he was on the verge of mental collapse, he ranted to himself. He watched the curve of her calf and recalled the many times he had lain in bed in the mornings and watched her dress for work. He had looked at the almost invisible roll of fat around her hips, the slight beginnings of buttocks sag that would eventually give her that pear-shaped figure she so valiantly strove to avoid with daily exercise.

He had read once somewhere that to test the firmness of breasts, you tried to keep a pencil in place beneath them. If the pencil fell, no problem. They had tried that experiment when she was thirty, and she had passed with flying colors. Now she was thirty-eight, and neither of them had brought up the tit exam for some time.

He was jerked from his reverie by a tug on his sleeve. "Hi, Dad." L.J. looked up at him with those big green eyes, her eyes, but he seemed hesitant. Larry had always been strict with his kids, and now that they had been without his authority for some time, he really didn't know how to approach them anymore.

He grabbed the boy and stood, hoisting him into the air like he had when they were both a lot younger. "Hello, Munchkin, how are you?"

The smile that finally crept out of the cherub face reminded Larry of the good times. "Steve's gonna win today, huh?"

"Believe it." Larry put L.J. down and watched Robyn approach. "How's your team doing?" he asked, without looking at the boy.

"Great. I finally hit the ball."

Larry took his gaze reluctantly from Robyn and smiled. "Fantastic!"

"Naw, hit it right into the first baseman's mitt."

Larry knelt and took the boy by the shoulders. "I told you, you got to keep your eye where you want the ball to go. How many times have I told you that?"

"A lot."

"Right. You have to learn to listen. You can do anything you want to do as long as you learn to listen to the people that know." He saw Robyn's shadow fall across L.J.'s face and suddenly he didn't want to confront her. "You want a hot dog or something?"

13

"Naw, I gorged out a little while ago." L.J. pivoted out of his father's grip and ran to the end of the line to watch his brother play.

"Hello, Larry." Robyn straightened her skirt and sat down on the bench beside him.

"Hi, babe, you're looking good."

"Thank you."

They sat in silence for a few minutes, both watching the action on the field. Larry lighted another cigarette and turned to his wife. "You're looking good."

"You said that."

"Yeah, well, you always said I was redundant," Larry remarked, with a little edge to his voice.

Robyn reached into her large leather purse and took out a pack of cigarettes. Larry fumbled for the lighter he had just put back into his pocket and had the three-inch butane flame flaring upward before she had a chance to open the fresh pack. Now, why the hell had he done that? He never lit her cigarette before.

She shook her head and he sat there like an idiot while she took her time tearing the cellophane from the pack with her long fingernails. "How's the new place? I hear you rented the Taj Mahal West."

"I rattle around in it quite a bit. And the lease is an elbow and a kneecap."

Robyn frowned. Larry could see it coming and sighed deeply. "You could have gotten something cheaper. You don't have to live like a feudal baron, you know."

"I have to live. You'd like to see me ensconced in some broken down studio apartment like—aw, shit, what the hell do you care anyway?"

"I care." She looked at him with that expression of concern that she used whenever she had his best interests at heart. He got ready to duck. "You don't live with someone for seventeen years and not care what happens

14

to them."

Now it's seventeen years. Pretty soon she'd have him believing they just celebrated their golden wedding anniversary.

The game began and they watched Steve's team kick off and carry the ball downfield toward the goal. Larry watched the action move away, then back again as the other team took possession of the ball. "You know what I think?" he said softly.

"What?"

"I don't think we really ever had anything. If we had, you wouldn't have walked away from it as easily as you did."

Robyn sighed. "We've been all through that."

"Well, let's go through it again!" Larry shouted. A few heads turned toward them, but Larry ignored the curious stares. "That 'personal growth' and 'self-recognition' bullshit is so trite I couldn't even use it in a script. You're hiding behind this 'be your own person' crap so you don't have to tell me the real reasons."

"You live in a fantasy world, Larry. You always have and you always will. It's that simple."

He grabbed her shoulder and turned her to face him. "Six months ago we were happily married. All of a sudden you get this hair up your ass about a trial separation. Okay, I went along with that. When you filed, I said, 'All right, there's still time for her to snap out of it.' Rob, the damn thing's going to be final soon. We're running out of time."

She pulled free of his grip. "Hah!"

"Hah, what?"

"Hah, happily married. You were happily married. You live on another planet, friend. You don't see anything real." She brushed at her eyes. "I don't want to talk about this anymore."

"Yeah, well, I think you'll find out someday, lady, that you made a big mistake." Larry rose and began to walk away.

"Where're you going?"

"To my fantasy world. I'll say hello to Peter Pan for you."

"You're going to leave your son's game when he really needs his father's support?"

Larry stopped and looked back at her. "I'm just his male parent. You're his father now."

The sun was going down as Larry slowed the Porsche to forty and turned onto his street with a squeal of rubber. He drove past the long rows of two-story town houses, each one containing two units and separated from the next identical wood and tan stucco structure by small patches of grass and desert rocks.

He downshifted into the cul-de-sac and hit the garage door opener on the dash. He was into the garage before the door was halfway up, and the car shuddered to a stop inches from the inside wall. Someday he was going to go right through into the kitchen, he knew. With his luck, he'd probably end up with the microwave oven in his lap and all his pubic hair would fall out.

The ground floor of the town house consisted of a large double-door entry hall that led to the step-down living room. Larry slammed the door and walked to the center of the living room, clenching his fists. To his right was the dining room, a long wet bar, and the kitchen. Behind him was the downstairs guest bath. The place was done in browns and blues. Thick chocolate carpeting covered all the floor area, creeping up the suspended stairs to the upper floor, which contained three bedrooms and two baths. Larry didn't need all that room, but it was the first place he had liked after looking at dozens, so he had snapped it up.

He had purchased all new furniture, brown and white striped sofas, wine keg end tables and a large antique chest coffee table. In one corner, near the long, raised-hearth fireplace, his TV set rested next to his component stereo and video recorder. He had planned to buy something to set all the equipment on, but hadn't gotten around to it yet.

He scowled at the plant in the hanging macrame basket that hung over the TV. It looked like it was on its last legs. He should water it once in a while, he guessed. He had bought a half-dozen healthy plants and placed them in ceramic pots and wicker baskets all through the house. He hadn't had much luck with them. As far as Larry was concerned, there were two types of plants: artificial and other people's.

He grabbed a beer from the bar refrigerator and plopped down on the sofa facing the dining room, studying the large oil painting above his desk. He didn't have a dining room set, so he used that area as his workroom. His desk, typewriter and stand, and two wooden bookcases filled it nicely, and he could look out the sliding glass doors at the cactus plants and ground cover in the back yard while he worked.

The painting looked eerie in the last rays of the setting sun that spilled in over the back fence and struck the wall. It was an original Stacin, a wide expanse of gray concrete with a long figure about the size of a man's thumb at its center. At both edges of the concrete that seemed to narrow to nothing in the distance were ruins of buildings. Above the glassy plain the sky was a mixture of gray haze and highlights of muted reds, as if there were more burning and destruction as far as the eye could see.

Larry sipped his beer and leaned back with his head against the wall, looking up at the high-beamed ceiling. He had been walking down the main street of Santa Cruz

17

one day eleven years ago. They had driven up to San Jose to visit Robyn's mother and he had gotten the urge to drive over the hill and walk on the beach. He had been locked in an ad agency job he hated and he needed to be alone to think.

He passed a small shop on Pacific Avenue, stopped and went back to peer in the window. The painting was the biggest thing in the shop, taking up the entire far wall of the narrow gallery. He had looked at it through the gritty glass for fifteen minutes before he got up the nerve to go inside and ask its price.

He drove a Camero convertible in those days and he had been forced to lower the top to get the painting in the back seat. All the way back to San Jose he had worried about Robyn's reaction to his latest crazy expenditure. He had good reason to be concerned.

"Where in God's name did you get such a depressing thing?" she had demanded when he took her out to the car to show her the painting.

"I like it."

"It's—it's gray. For Christ sake, how will we get it home?"

They drove all the way back with the top down, the painting wrapped in brown butcher paper in the back seat, sticking up like an embarrassing erection. She hated to get windblown and cooked at the same time, and maybe that was the reason she never liked the picture. They had been living in the house in Hawthorne at the time, and he hung it in the living room above the fireplace. When they moved to Northridge after L.J. was born, she did the main room in crystal and mirrors and the painting was relegated to the family room with the pool table and the TV set, the other two items of furniture to which she also took a great distaste.

The next year he had started to write for TV and she

convinced him to hang it in the bedroom because they were entertaining a lot. That was the year she talked him into selling the pool table.

The picture graced the wall above the bed for less than six months before she decided to wallpaper, and for some reason it ended up "temporarily" in the garage covered with an old Air Force blanket. Now it hung in a place of honor on a wide white wall, its carved wood frame polished with lemon oil. He had reclined on the sofa many a night recently and looked at it, finally understanding why he liked it so much.

He was that lone figure at its center.

TWO

The *Two Families* business offices were located in a long white building behind the permanent sets on BarRon's back lot. Larry parked in the space with his name painted in large red letters early the next morning and entered the building. He walked down the long hall done in basket-weave wallpaper and pushed through a door that bore the inscription: WRITERS. Somebody had scribbled beneath the plaque in blue crayon: PSYCH I.C.U. METHAPHORICAL PARADOXES RESOLVED WHILE YOU WAIT.

He was greeted by a cloud of smoke that circled Lew Beckerman's head like Pig Pen's perennial dust cloud. The heavy-set writer sat at his desk at one end of the long room that was furnished with two other, larger desks, an assortment of chairs that looked extremely comfortable but ragged, several TV sets, and a Lanier computer keyboard terminal. Beckerman looked up, smiled around the fat cigar in his mouth, and nodded his bushy head. "Hey, the prodigal son. Finally decided to show up, huh?"

Larry walked to the long row of file cabinets that lined one wall. "For awhile, anyway."

The third member of the writing team looked up from her seat at the computer. "Stop by to do some work, or

20

just passing through?" Patte Gordon was a wispy, elflike woman in her mid-thirties. She weighed ninety-five pounds dressed in chain mail, and she was by far the prettiest member of the Magnanimous Trio, as they called themselves.

"Got a meeting with Benny Frankel in an hour," Larry grunted as he sorted through the mess in the drawer. "Beat the puzzle today?" He was referring to Patte's constant battle with the *Variety* crossword puzzle.

"Need a four letter word—"

"You're asking the right guy," Lew interjected with his usual idiotic grin. He was twenty-seven, the youngest writer on the staff, and he had the kind of quick wit Larry admired above all else.

"A four letter word," she continued, "for Naval deposit." Patte scowled at Lew.

"Lint," Larry said casually, pulling a bound script from the cabinet. "You see, Flash, your problem is that you capitalize everything. You probably tried to fit *depth charge* in there, right?"

"Wrong. I used *torp*."

"Figures," Larry sighed.

"What's with Frankel?" Lew asked.

"He's still trying to sell that loan-shark script," Patte said to Lew. "A more horrible concept I never saw."

"I'm glad you write better than you talk, lady," Larry chided.

"Does she?" laughed Lew. "I hadn't noticed."

Larry leaned on the cabinet and curled the script in his hands. "Well, maybe this time we can put a deal together. You guys doing okay?"

Patte frowned, which gave her the appearance of an angry leprechaun. "Mitch'll be here in half an hour. He has some comments about the first draft of the Christmas two-parter."

Mitchell Donovan was one of the stars of *Two Families*, and he was to try his hand at directing the two-parter. "God save us from actors who think they can direct," Larry said to the ceiling.

"Amen to that." Lew puffed blue smoke into the air. "Before you know it, they'll want to write too."

Larry went over the messages on his desk, tossing them one by one into a large wastebasket. "What's the problem?"

"We need to run through some final changes for next week." Patte flipped open a red folder.

"Shoot. I got a few minutes."

Lew smiled and sat back, eyes narrowed. "We work on this sucker for thirty-six hours straight, and you waltz in here at the eleventh hour and do magic, huh?"

Larry looked up. "That's why I get the big bucks."

"Okay." Patte found the page she was looking for. "When Felicia's talking to Bob, she says: 'Are you a mind reader?' Lew and I think Karen should come in with something there to zing him again. Whatta you think?"

"Hmmm." Larry thought for a moment. "How 'bout if she just gives him her usual exasperated look. You know, that picture and a thousand words crap?"

"Wait a minute—I got it!" Patte exclaimed. Her face lighted up like a wino had just discovered a case of Chevas in the garbage. Larry loved to see her react like that. They worked well together, all three of them. "Karen looks at Felicia, points a thumb at Bob and says: 'To the schlep here, mental telepathy is a method U.S. Steel developed for refining ore over a long distance.'"

Larry and Lew both grinned. "Not bad, Flash."

"Wasn't meant to be," Patte said demurely.

"Okay, let's go with that. What else?"

"When Karen's talking about her ex-mother-in-law. Let's see—"

"Page eight." Lew took the cigar from between his teeth and leaned forward.

"Yeah, right." Patte turned to the page. "She says: 'The old bat was so neat she put doggie bags beside each plate at dinner.'"

"That sucks," Larry reflected. "Who came up wth that clunker?"

"You," Lew and Patte echoed in unison.

"Oh. On second thought—"

Lew scratched his head. "How about: 'She was so neat when she heard there was a burglar in the neighborhood, she polished the silver?'"

Larry groaned. "That's lousy."

"Better than the other one," Patte said.

"Okay, put it in. Both of you owe me one." Larry rose and headed for the door. "See, you guys don't really need me. You do just fine on your own."

Patte made a face at him. "Your very presence inspires us to creativity, sir. Without you, we'd just sit around and watch our socks sag."

Larry fished his briefcase out of a pile of magazines on the floor and put the script inside. Patte turned to Lew. "Okay, Felicia asks—very sexy—as if she's about to melt: 'How do you like your women?' How does Bob respond?"

Lew nodded through the haze around his head. "'I like my women like my eggs, sunny side up.'"

"Not bad." Patte scribbled on a pad while Larry reached for the doorknob. "Whatta ya think?"

Larry called back, "Have him say: 'I like 'em over easy.' It's more in character."

"My God, the man's a genius." Lew scowled.

"But he's right." Patte grinned.

Larry opened the door and gave them an Errol Flynn wave. "See you gentlemen later."

Patte stuck her tongue out at the reference to her sex.

"You asshole."

Larry gave her a broad grin. "And you, my dear, are a crunt."

"What's a crunt?"

"Oh, oh," Lew laughed. "You walked right into that one, Gordon."

"A crunt, my dear, is a vagina with teeth. You're the only woman I know who douches with Colgate."

Patte brightened and looked at Lew. "Hey, can we use that? I mean just the douching with toothpaste bit?"

"Fuck no," Lew answered.

"Sure you can," Larry chimed in. "Stick it in and let the Standards and Practices boys yank it. That way we can get the 'over easy' line past them."

Patte nodded at Lew. "You're right, the man is a genius."

"Anytime." Larry smiled as he closed the door.

Benny Frankel's office was on the tenth floor of the Glendale Savings Building at the corner of Wilshire and Beverly Drive. In the underground garage Larry watched the attendant screech away in his Porsche. He winced at the sound of rubber on cement as he walked to the elevators. He punched the up button and peered around a pillar, trying to catch a glimpse of the Porsche that was now a streak of crimson on the other side of the garage.

An elderly man in a business suit strolled up behind him and laughed. "You just have to turn your back and walk away from it."

"What?" The statement took Larry by surprise.

"Only way to keep sane." The man nodded at another attendant that was running toward a car for a Le Mans start. "I keep seeing visions of my Citroen splattered all over the north turn."

Larry smiled weakly and entered the elevator as the

door opened. Getting out on ten, he walked down the long hall to the outer office of RedEye Productions. A buxom young receptionist he knew only as Karen greeted him. "Hi, Mr. DiAMonte. Benny's on the phone, but I'll buzz him you're here."

"The hell with Benny. I came to see you. How 'bout dinner and some foolin' around?" With the kind of luck he was having lately, she'd probably say yes and he'd end up with Herpes.

"Hmmm, I don't know. What would your wife say?" She smiled up at him with an expression that said, You're not a bad guy, fella, just too old for me.

"I'm not married anymore," he blurted out, too defensively, he decided, after he said it.

"Oh yeah? Why you still wearing a wedding band then?"

Larry looked down at his hand. Sure enough, the ring, a wide silver band inset with turquoise and coral, stared back at him like a neon sign. Why the hell was he still wearing it? Force of habit? He had refused to wear a wedding band when they were first married, but Robyn had spotted this pair in a little shop in Monterey one weekend and convinced him he was wrong. Had she worn hers today? He couldn't remember.

Karen looked up from the intercom. "You can go in now, Mr. DiAMonte."

"Huh? Oh, yeah. See you later." He walked to the doorway.

"Hey," Karen called after him. He turned. "Try wearing it on the other hand."

Benny Frankel came out from behind a massive desk piled high with manuscripts and books and met him with outstretched hands. He was a young man, barely thirty, with sandy, thinning hair and a beach-boy quality to his deeply tanned face. Larry had only known him for a short time, but Frankel had the same perverted sense of humor

25

and the two men got along well. "How the hell are you? Heard any good ones lately?"

They shook hands. "Heard any? I write 'em. You're looking fit. How's Emily?"

Benny chuckled and moved back to his large swivel chair. Larry took a seat in front of the desk, script in his lap, the bound folder feeling more like hat in hand. "She moved out," Benny said. "Got a new one, name's Jennifer. You'll love her—all tits and ass and absolutely no personality."

"Well, they say likes attract, huh?"

"You son of a bitch. You expect me to listen kindly to your proposal after that?"

Larry leaned back in the chair and smiled. "You want to hear my latest producer joke or not?"

"Fire when ready, Gridley."

"Okay, budget's just been set and the producer's talking to the casting director. He says: 'I want the top name in the industry for this film. We'll pay five mil, that's max. I want you to get me John Wayne.' The CD pales and says: 'But R.M., he's—he's dead!' The producer scratches his head and considers the statement for a minute. Then, with a penetrating look, he says: 'Okay, *six* mil, but not a penny more.'"

Benny broke up. "That's poor. Oh, is that gross."

"Yeah, and you'll be telling it at a party tonight, right?"

"You bet your ass." Benny propped his chin between his hands and leaned forward, his elbows on the desk. "You ever think about writing short paragraphs for big money?" he inquired innocently.

"Fuck you, Frankel. You want to hear the story idea or not?"

"If you insist on wasting my time again with another *Invasion of the Bodice Snatchers*."

"This one's a winner," Larry guaranteed.

26

"That's what you said the last two times. Tell me something?"

"Sure."

"Why do you fool with this stuff?" Benny waved at the pile of scripts that looked like they were about to topple from his desk top. "You're a hot TV writer. You found your niche and you're good at what you do. Who needs this aggravation?"

"Would you believe I could be the next Neil Simon?"

"Yeah, I'd believe that. But then I backed Jimmy Carter in '76, so I'll believe anything."

Larry sighed. "I dunno, I just think there's got to be more to it than writing tripe for thirteen weeks and running with the money. Besides, there's people out there I'm gonna show. Know what I mean?"

"Yep, been showing them all my life. All right, now that you managed to mellow me out of my usual critical mood, lay the story on me before I start to cry." Benny leaned back and put his hands behind his head.

"Right. Picture if you will—"

Benny groaned and let his eyes close. Larry continued, "Picture if you will an extreme close-up of an alien monster, terrible, frightening, ugly."

"My second wife," Benny muttered.

"Shut up and let me tell it, or so help me, I'll take it to Zanuck and Brown. Okay, we got this horrible monstrosity, right? Its face contorts and it says in a Bronx accent so thick it'd make Archie Bunker sound like William Buckley: 'So how's your brudder?'" Benny's brow furrowed and Larry knew what he was thinking. A sci-fi comedy is just what the world really needs, friend. It would outgross *Abbott and Costello Go to Mars.*

"We pull back to see the interior of a trailer, and the thing in the chair is being made up by the ace brush man in the business."

27

"Hmmm." Benny nodded, but kept his eyes closed. Larry had him hooked and they both knew it.

"Our main character, the makeup man, tells his captive audience about his crazy kid brother, a twenty-five year old stuntman who's having a hard time growing up between the horses and the broads. We establish the protectiveness of the older brother and then go to the two of them after work. The kid tells him he's in deep shit with the local Shylock and needs five grand to bail himself out. The brother is loaded, but thinks the kid needs a lesson, so he tells him no.

"They leave the house they share a few mornings later, and their car blows up, killing the kid and fucking up our hero royally. He wakes up a week later in the hospital to find out his brother is dead and his hands are so bad he may never work again.

"Then we bring in our female lead, a lady police lieutenant who tells our boy—let's call him Harry for the sake of perspective—"

"Why Harry?" Benny asked cautiously.

"'Cause that's the sucker's name."

"I'll buy that."

"So she tells Harry they got a good idea who smoked the car, but no proof. Harry is out of his skull with grief and guilt. He's gonna get the bastards that did it, no matter how long it takes." Larry paused for breath.

"Well, go on, for Christ sake!"

Larry smiled and rose. He strode back and forth in front of the desk, gesturing with his hands, knowing Benny was peeking through his lashes. Might as well give it his best, for the meek shall inherit the daytime soaps. "Harry goes through a grueling recuperation, getting back partial use of his hands. The story line is his masterful use of disguises to bring the loan-shark organization to its knees. He does a black pimp, an old lady, a double amputee, a beat-up

28

hooker, and with the use of his talent and thirst for revenge he succeeds in getting the syndicate to kill each other off in ways that I, in all humility, can only describe as very cineramic. Of course we bring in the girl from time to time. He falls for her, but they're both working toward the same end through totally different means. There's a couple of neat car chases and all the other ingredients necessary to make it a very desirable project."

"What's it called?" Benny asked. Larry couldn't tell if his tone showed interest or disgust.

"*Five'll Get You Ten.*"

"Catchy title."

"Would that we could sell titles."

Benny opened his eyes all the way and smiled. "I have on several occasions. Who else has seen this?"

"Nobody."

"You and me go back a long way, ole buddy. So don't put me on the high-all."

"We go back ten months, pal. And I certainly would stroke you if I thought it would do any good. But in this case you're getting first look."

Benny reached across the desk and took the script from Larry's grasp. He balanced it in the palm of his hand as if its weight would tell him how strong a concept it was. "Okay, I'll give it a read and get back to you."

"When?"

"When? Yom Kippur. How the hell do I know when? Look at all this shit." He gestured at the pile of unread material on his desk in disgust.

Larry placed both hands on the desk top and leaned in. "Two weeks. Then I make a dozen copies and take one to everybody. Understand?" Larry was fishing. If Frankel was really intersted in the script he would agree to the deadline. Of course, if he wasn't interested, he might agree anyway.

"You got it." Benny rose and walked to the door with Larry. They shook hands. "How's Robyn and the kids?"

"Robyn who?"

"That bad, huh?"

"Hey, just read the script. You know where to reach me." Larry shut the door, leaving Benny Frankel standing there with the folder in his hands. Frankel went back to his desk, sat, and opened it to page one.

THREE

An alto sax batted out the low strains of "Cherry Pink and Apple Blossom White" from the twin three-foot-high conical speakers on either side of the fireplace. A brown Indian-design throw blanket was spread in front of the high used-brick hearth. The only light in the room came from the mosaic of dancing flames that reflected off the beamed ceiling, tracing a latticework of shadows on the thick rug.

Larry was on his back on the blanket, his head resting on a large blue pillow that was braced against the hearth. He was naked, his legs spread wide apart, his hips slightly elevated by another smaller pillow.

Branda sat between his legs, her long black hair falling down her bare back to her hips. She had exceptionally long legs, nice full hips, but breasts a little small for Larry's taste. Not that he was complaining. She was a good kid and she knew all the moves. She even worked without a net.

He had met her in church. The last time he had been in church was for L.J.'s christening. When the priest had made some remark about driving the devil away, Larry had leaned back against the wall of the rectory, nudging one of the long-handled money baskets. It had fallen, hitting the

31

long row of other baskets, and they had come down on everybody's heads like a row of dominoes. It wasn't a burning bush, but it was a clear sign to Larry, and he hadn't returned until Ned Vickers, the producer of *Two Families,* had gotten married last month.

They had danced at the reception and he had taken her home with him. Since that first encounter, he had dated her regularly, at least twice a week. She was secretary for a talent agent in town, not the brightest girl he had ever met, but she sure bolstered the hell out of his sagging macho image.

Right now she was doing what he liked best, rubbing his left calf with one hand while she held his engorged penis flat to his stomach with the long fingers of her other hand, massaging the frenulum of her Petcock, as she liked to call it. She sure had a way with words, but Larry wasn't worrying all that much about her creative vocabulary as she applied a two-finger pressure to the very sensitive area on the dorsal surface just below the coronal ridge. He moaned appreciatively and arched his back so he could enjoy the full effect of her ministrations.

"Feel good?" Branda inquired with a teasing smile, as she used the palm of her hand to move his penis in wide arc across his stomach muscles. He just sighed and lifted his buttocks higher. She laughed, then leaned to one side. Using both hands she rolled his rigid cock between them like a Boy Scout attempting to start a fire with a stick. He liked that and his increased moaning assured her he was on the brink of an orgasm. "Getting close, honey?"

"Uh-huh."

Her smile broadened, and she grabbed his hips tightly, taking him almost completely into her mouth. Holding on firmly, she went to her side, pulling him over her. He straddled her, his knees to either side of her shoulders, his hands braced on the hearth for support. This was his favorite position and she knew it. He loved feeding her his cock like this, loved the way she kept her eyes open and watched his glistening shaft slide in and out of her mouth. Christ, she was going to go cross-eyed if he thrust it in any further, but he didn't voice that thought for fear of breaking her up and interrupting the mood.

Working her hands between his thighs, she grabbed his penis and began pumping it into her mouth with long strokes, removing it completely with the outward motion so that she could run her tongue across its head and murmur to him. "I want . . . you . . . to come . . . in my mouth."

Her speech was somewhat robotic because of the fleshy impediment, but that didn't bother him. What troubled him was the fact he was thinking of Robyn, wondering what she was doing at this very moment. Was she engaged in similar acrobatics with her lover, the business associate she had been sleeping with for the last year and a half? "Hmmm . . . tastes . . . so good."

He'd better not think about that anymore or he was going to lose his erection. Just because she had dumped him for another guy, a real loser at that, was no reason he shouldn't enjoy himself. No reason to let that get to him. Then why *did* it? "Fuck," he said aloud.

"Yes . . ." Branda moaned, then sucked him in deeply. Pulling him violently from her mouth, she licked the head of his penis like a little girl enjoying an ice cream cone. "Fuck me in the mouth . . . now . . ."

He stiffened his torso and dug his toes into the rug. Lifting his knees from the floor, he braced himself on his hands and feet; the only connection between the two of them was his shaft of flesh. That seemed somehow symbolic to him, even though they now closely resembled two aircraft in the process of midflight refueling.

She stroked her breasts with her hands and sucked hard

33

as he did pushups, never taking her eyes from his. Unable to hold back any longer, he came. As soon as she felt the warmth spurting into her mouth, she let out a massive sigh, as if she had just had an oral orgasm. She brought her hands up again and began pumping him vigorously, letting his cock slide from her mouth, then running it back and forth over her parted lips, his semen dripping from her mouth and coating her cheeks and chin as her tongue darted from side to side to lick at the milky substance.

Larry finally relaxed and fell to his side, easing the pained muscles in his back and legs. Branda held on and pushed him over on his back. They lay there for a few moments while she massaged the semen into his skin and then licked him dry. "Was that good?" she asked, running her tongue across her lips and smiling.

"On a scale of one to seventy, babe, that was definitely a sixty-nine."

"Hmmm." She snuggled into his arms and put her head against his chest. "Gonna let me spend the night?"

"Can't do. Gotta work."

"Aww, come on, that's what you always say. For once, let's just do crazy things all night."

Larry pushed her gently to one side and reached for a pair of Levi's on the floor. Pulling them on, he tossed her the dress from the back of a chair. "Maybe next time."

Branda pouted, but slipped into her clothing. Larry picked up her purse and walked her out down the long path that led to the driveway with his arm around her waist. As he opened her car door for her, a new BMW sedan pulled into the next driveway. Branda waved and backed out as the BMW pulled into the adjoining garage. Larry got a glimpse of his next-door neighbor as she got out of her car. She was tall, maybe thirty-five, and her medium-length auburn hair framed the classical features of her face. Before he could study her further, she hit the switch on the wall and the door began to descend. He felt like going to his knees to peek at her as the door came down, but that was silly. Although she sure looked like the most beautiful woman he had ever seen.

The next morning Larry walked on the *Two Families* set looking for Ned Vickers. The producer had left a note on Larry's desk about some script changes, and Larry wound his way through the miling crew looking for him. The set was laid out in the center of the sound stage, a long line of open rooms, the top floors of both duplexes adjoining the bottom floors with the driveways and lawns on the other side of the stage. Outdoor shots were taken on location at a similar set of buildings in Burbank, but Larry seldom left the compressed atmosphere of the sound stage.

Larry spotted Vickers standing next to a grip who was wielding an electric saw, cutting a hole in a wall of the upstairs bedroom of the left duplex. It was the scene where Bob, mad with lust for his ex-wife, decides he was going to take whatever measures were necessary to get to her. Funny bit, if I do say so myself, Larry mused. Hell, if he didn't, who would?

Vickers was an extremely tall man, thin and balding. He wore a perpetually grim expression along with his sneakers, Levi's and a sweatshirt. He was the studio production chief and president of BarRon Productions. He had ankled MGM-TV a year ago to go into production on his own, and *Two Families* was his first major show. He ws very concerned about its success, and most of the time he let everybody involved share that concern.

Larry waved and Vickers muttered some instructions to the man with the saw and walked over. "You the exec story consultant or what?" Vickers scowled as he spat out

35

the words.

"No . . . I'm the Vice-President of the United States. If I mentioned my name you'd probably recognize it."

"Very funny."

"That's what you pay me for, pal. What's the problem this time?"

Vickers gestured to a youngish script girl named Madeline. She walked over and handed him a hefty folder. He stuck it under Larry's nose and fanned the pages. "See the virtual rainbow of hues that abound here?" He was referring to the rewrite pages that were done in different colors every time a revision was made. "I'm up to my asshole in changes and I haven't seen you in two days. So how's Branda?"

"Brutal. And the new bride?"

"She's got this old man hopping. I'm thinking about taking up necrophilia. Wanna join the L.A. chapter?"

"Naw, I'll limit myself to the walking wounded if you don't mind. I've always thought necrophilia was sexist."

Vickers laughed. "You got a point there." He shoved the script into Larry's hands. "See if you can do something with scene eight. It works beautifully when Karen crawls into bed with Bob, thinking he's her new husband, but Mitch is unhappy about the lack of dialogue the next morning when she discovers who he really is.

"The reaction shots are all we need, damn it. When she stretches and smiles at him, then does a take as he grins like a banshee, that's pure poetry. The look on her face when she realizes she's been had again is a work of art.

"Mitch feels it's his scene, and he should have a line there. You want to talk to him or what? Our poor director just threw his clipboard at me and ran out screaming."

"We don't need a line there, Ned," said Larry.

Vickers put one arm around Larry's shoulder and nodded in agreement. "Right. Talk to him anyway, will ya?"

"Where is he?"

Vickers stuck a thumb at the ceiling. Larry frowned and walked away, holding the script. That, my friend, is why you want to write movies, he assured himself. So you don't have to deal with prima donnas every day of your life. Something in the back of his mind told him that there might be a prima donna or two in the film industry also, but he just ignored the nagging thought.

He found Mitchell Donovan on the roof of the sound stage, having a cup of coffee and a Danish. He was wearing a bathing suit and lounging in a chaise reading a *TV Guide*. Donovan was a good-looking man, well muscled and craggy. He had a magnificent smile, and he aimed it at Larry as he waved the magazine at another deck chair. Larry noticed it was the copy with Mitch's face gracing the cover.

"Did you see this?"

Larry settled into the deck chair and sighed. "Who could miss it? You bought two hundred copies and autographed them for everybody you could catch."

Mitch ignored the remark and folded the magazine to a back page. "Listen to this." He began reading. "'Mitchell Donovan is essentially a loner. To an interviewer, he once said, "I have to be alone because I'm better than ninety-two percent of the people out there." Donovan has come a long way. It used to be one hundred percent.'"

Larry grabbed half the Danish from the paper plate on the small glass table and stuffed it into his mouth as Donovan continued. "Now get this: 'A fellow actor on *Two Families,* Sam Briedbart, suggested that he start doing talk shows so that more people could get to know the real Donovan, the humble, shy, sensitive man who was hiding beneath that smoke screen of vanity and conceit. To this he replied, "Bull—!"'"

37

Donovan laughed and punched Larry on the shoulder. "Ain't it the truth?"

"I want to talk to you about the bedroom scene." Larry attempted to change the subject.

Donovan ignored him and resumed reading. "'But he is all of the above, especially his proclivity in referring to steer manure at the slightest provocation, and he freely admits it, boasting that star quality consists of being able to effectively display a wide variety of emotions.'" Donovan pointed the magazine at Larry. "Well? What do you think? Did they capture the real me?"

The only way they could capture the real you, friend, he thought, is with a butterfly net. Instead, he said, "About the bedroom scene, Mitch—"

"Yeah, I was thinking I should deliver a socko line there."

Socko? Jesus Christ, the man was reading the trades again. "Mitch, you want a line there, you got it. If you want to recite the Gettysburg Address, I'll paraphrase it for you."

"That's not funny."

"That's just the point, it isn't funny. Funny is when you just sit there, peek over the top of the newspaper and give her that ole shit-eatin' grin that's made you a household word. Believe me, if I could have come up with a line that would have made the scene funnier, I would have." Larry leaned forward and gave Donovan his number one sincere look. "What we're going for here, Mitch, is the whole idea. The conceptual approach is called ensemble acting. That means the interaction of a group of distinctive actors working together to make a great show, rather than concentrated individual effort."

Sure, it sounded hokey even to Larry, but that was the way he knew the show should go and damned if he was going to let Donovan fuck it up. "If I give you a line there, then everybody's going to be on my back to expand their parts. The trick is to be outstanding with the least amount of dialogue, you know, like Newman or McQueen. Just like Brando, huh? You can understand Brando, can't you?"

Donovan considered Larry's words for a full minute before replying. "Brando, huh?"

"You bet your ass."

"I still think I need a line there."

Larry was getting ready to find out if a man could drown in half a cup of coffee when Donovan smiled and said, "If you think it's right, I'll trust you. But you owe me one, DiaMonte, so let me read you the rest of the article."

Larry rose. "I don't owe you that much. See you later."

Back downstairs Madeline handed him a slip of paper as he strode across the set. He looked down and read it as he walked. "Your wife phoned. Said it was important." He crumpled the note and tossed it in a trash can as he passed. Going into the corridor that led to the offices, he put a dime in a payphone on the wall and punched out his home number. He didn't expect her to be at the house, but maybe one of the kids would answer. After a dozen rings he hung up, realizing that it was a school day and too early for anybody to be home.

He called her office number. It must have been her floor day, because she answered the phone herself. "Frazier Realty, this is Robyn DiaMonte." Her voice had the usual sparkling quality he had come to know so well, similar to that of a circus barker he had once heard as a child.

"It's me. What ya want?"

"We need to talk."

"We talked. I'm busy."

"About support."

"You got to be kidding. The marital agreement was specific. Nobody gets nothin' from nobody."

"Things are getting tight."

"F'chrissake, you make more than I do!" Larry screamed into the phone. Why did he always end up yelling at her? She remained so fucking calm and he always ended up shouting.

"In case you haven't heard, we're in a recession. Interest rates are through the roof and mortgage money is almost unobtainable. Very few people are buying."

Larry smiled. "Gee, that's too bad, babe. I seem to recall statements like, 'I don't need anything from you, I can make it on my own,' and so forth." There was a silence on the line. Finally Larry said, "Why don't you get your lover to support you. He's a real pillar of strength."

Robyn sighed deeply. "Let's leave Lee out of this."

"I would have liked to. Look. As my sainted mother used to say, 'You mada you bed, fuck ina it.' I'll be a son of a bitch if I'd give you a dime to call the fire department if your hair was in flames!"

"You'll never change, you know that? I thought there was hope, but I guess I was just dreaming."

"Oh, I've changed, babe. I've joined the Israeli Air Force."

"What?"

"I've become a Jewish fighter pilot. They can't lose because they don't give a shit."

"You're insane." She was beginning to sob. Larry felt sorry for her, so he offered a suggestion. "Why don't you grab somebody with money, instead of that deadbeat you hooked up with? You know all the moves, use them while you still got the looks. Find yourself a rich divorce attorney. Hey, I'll give you the name of mine."

There was a *click* as Robyn hung up on him. "By the way, lover," he said into the dead phone. "I'd like my name back, if you don't mind."

FOUR

Larry drove home that afternoon, the phone conversation with Robyn still churning his guts. Why couldn't the damn woman just leave him alone? He didn't want to talk to her, see her, think about her. He didn't want to know her any more. He looked up at the sky through the T-top of his car. Was that too much to ask? He wasn't wrong, she was a coldblooded opportunist. A scheming, conniving bitch. Their last night together had proven that.

The hard irony of the situation was that they were still sleeping in the same bed. No sex for the last six weeks, but every night he had to climb in and lay there beside her, wondering what the hell she was thinking, hoping that she would reach out and touch his arm and give him some indication that she needed him as badly as he needed her.

He always slept in the nude, regardless of the temperature, and he continued even though she bundled up in her most unattractive nightgowns.

That night he had padded out of the bathroom with a partial erection and looked over at her. She was sitting at the dressing table applying a liberal coating of Noxema to her face. He hated the smell because it was like a signal flag. The nights she donned the cream before getting into bed meant there would be no sex.

He was feeling miserable as he climbed into bed. Tomorrow morning he would be moving into his new place. He would be leaving his home of ten years for good. He would be uprooted from the surroundings that made him feel secure and plunged into the Unknown.

The marital agreement had been signed two weeks ago, and the division of community property was complete. She was to keep the house and the other three pieces of real estate they owned jointly and cash him out with the money they had in the savings accounts. But that wasn't enough to pay him for his share of the equities, so before he would sign the quit claims, she deeded him a second on the house in Hawthorne for the difference. She hadn't been ecstatic about that. She didn't like the idea of sending him a monthly check, but it was either that or sell everything, and she refused to part with property she claimed would appreciate ten to twenty percent a year.

"You come out of this smelling like a rose," she had told him several times in the last few days. "And I've got to scrape along hand to mouth wondering how I'm going to feed the kids."

Well, fuck you, lady. This was all your idea. But it got to him even if he didn't let it show. He was worried about her and the kids. Sure, she had demonstrated an uncanny ability to earn the big bucks. That still surprised him, although he inwardly believed she'd fall on her face without him. Maybe he hoped she'd go down in flames and come crawling back to him, pleading for another chance.

He had fantasied about that reunion many times, how he would graciously forgive her and come off looking like the Pope. But he hadn't known about her lover then. He had accepted her statements that she needed to be on her own in order to become a complete person, and not to remain secondary to his dominant personality, as she put it.

He had never cheated on her, not in all those years. And God knew he had been given plenty of opportunity. Yeah, he had lusted in his heart, his mind, his groin. Maybe he had cheated. Maybe coveting was the same thing.

She turned off the night stand lamp and slipped into bed beside him. He had his head braced by two pillows, and she always slept on her back, so they both lay there staring at the dark ceiling. After a few moments of uncomfortable silence Larry rose and opened the drapes in front of the long glass doors. There was no moon, but he switched on the pool lights, and the green-white glow made dancing shadows on the bed. He stood there looking out at the manicured back yard with its bathhouse and hot tub, knowing that she was watching his naked form and hoping it might spark some sort of reaction.

They had made love many times in the light from the pool because she thought it was romantic. Maybe some old memories would stir. He stood up straight and turned slightly so that his back was to her. She had always liked his ass. She had told him he had the nicest buns she ever saw. She could never resist grabbing his cheeks and squeezing until he yelled for help. Yep, the old beautiful buttocks routine might save the day.

"Are you coming to bed or going for a swim?" So much for ass power, he thought, as he looked back at her over his shoulder. She was smiling. Somewhere over the last four years—he couldn't put his finger on the exact time it happened—she had lost the smile he had loved so much. In the old days she would grin, showing her even white teeth, her eyes widening with a look of perpetual innocence that melted his insides. Now she smiled thin-lipped, mouth closed, corners of her eyes narrowed to the point of squinting. It almost made her ugly. Almost.

It wasn't just him, she smiled at everybody that way. When had the woman-child he married, the soft baby he had cuddled and protected and looked after, when had she become a stranger? "Yeah, I guess I'm coming to bed." He got back in between the sheets, but he left the pool lights on.

"Tomorrow you'll be on your own," he said, after a while.

"It's not going to be easy for either of us." There was a small catch in her voice, he thought, or maybe he was hearing it because he wanted it to be there. He had the crazy urge to reach over and take her in his arms and squeee her tightly to his chest.

Instead, he said, "Don't suppose you'd consider going for a sympathy fuck for Auld Lang Syne?" It was funny and she laughed. He hadn't wanted her to laugh. That was one of his problems. He used humor to mask his real emotions, a shield against reality, she had always said. She was probably right.

"No," she said seriously. "I couldn't do that. It would bring back all the old feelings, and I can't handle that anymore."

He rolled over on his side to face her. "Look at it this way. We can pretend we're strangers. Trust me."

She shook her head and pulled the covers up to her chin, a little girl gesture that reminded him of the first years of their marriage. He stayed on his side, watching her profile in the wavering light. He had the desire to grab her and press his body against hers, hoping that he still had the power to arouse her. The way his luck was running, he'd probably throw his back out.

"I think it'd be best if you waited till after the kids left for school before you took your stuff out. It's going to be hard enough on them as it is."

44

"Yeah." He really didn't have all that much to take. He had to buy all new furniture; and his desk, books, typewriter, and clothing were the sum total of all his possessions. And the painting. Mustn't forget the painting.

Whoever said, A man should not acquire more worldly goods than he can carry in his hands at a dead run, must have been a very sage individual—or somebody's ex-husband. "You gonna be okay?" he asked suddenly.

"It's going to be hard for the next month or so, till a couple of my escrows close . . ." She let the statement trail off and the guilt set in.

It did. "You need a few bucks to tide you over?" He asked the question out of the old protection reflex, knowing that he'd regret it.

"It's going to be difficult with you taking all the cash. Wouldn't hurt you to contribute a little something to your children's welfare."

Larry sighed. "How much do you need?"

"Four thousand would keep my head above water."

He sat bolt upright in the bed. "Four grand? Are you nuts?"

"Well, maybe I could get by on thirty-five hundred," she said sweetly.

Okay, roll over, face the wall and go to sleep before you end up carrying all your worldly goods in one hand, he told himself. Instead of taking his own outstanding advice, he said, "Out of the question."

They lay there in silence for a few minutes, Larry wondering if she had gone to sleep, afraid to look over at her. Then he felt her hand on his bare shoulder. "Maybe we could work something out." Her fingers moved up to caress his neck.

"Are you suggesting that I pay you to make love with me?"

There was a sharp intake of breath from the other side

of the bed. "No. I'm suggesting that we've been a lot to each other. I'm suggesting that if you were to do something kind for me, it wouldn't be hard to reciprocate."

"That's a lot of money for a piece of ass, Rob."

She pulled away. "You caustic bastard! Every time I think you're acting like a decent human being, you have to prove otherwise. You'll never change!"

Larry reached over and touched her cheek with the back of his hand. "How about a thousand?"

"I'm not going to bargain with you. If you can't do something nice for once in your life, then you can go to hell for all I care!"

Larry considered the situation. The money wasn't that important, and maybe she was trying to tell him something the only way she knew how. "Okay," he said softly.

"Okay what?"

"Okay, I'm making you a gift of thirty-five hundred bucks, no strings attached, out of the goodness of my heart."

"Four." She began stroking his thigh.

"All right, dammit!"

Robyn rose and began to slip out of her nightgown. She stood beside the bed in the light from the pool and let the straps fall seductively from her shoulders. The gown dropped to the floor, revealing her wide nipples, then her flat stomach, and finally the thin line of dark hair between her thighs.

Larry had a full erection before the nightgown settled to the rug. Talk about Pavlov's dogs. He would salivate when she so much as winked at him. "You want to write me a check?" she asked, as she stood there sucking in her stomach, her hands on his hips, her breasts protruding in his direction, tantalizing him.

"Now?" Larry asked incredulously.

46

He studied her face in the half-light from the pool. She looked plastically attractive in the flickering glow, like a manikin that had been granted life for a few brief moments. Her hair fell away from her high forehead and her mouth was slighly open and her eyes were glazed. She looked like a picture Larry had once seen in the newspaper, a photograph of a corpse published for identification purposes. You know the person is dead, but somehow you can't really be sure.

She was a mime, just going through the motions. He knew then he'd never get her back this way.

She pressed down hard on his penis, contracting her plexus muscles, an exercise she had practiced religiously since the birth of their last child, after her gynecologist told her it was a good way to keep toned. That was all it took. He came in sharp, almost painful waves, holding the cheeks of her ass tightly with both hands, as if he were afraid she'd move away before he was finished.

They had completed the act without exchanging a word and he wanted her to remain on top of him for a while, but she was beginning to get uncomfortable. She arched her back and let his slippery penis slide out, always wanting to break clean, never wanting to get his semen on her legs.

She fell to her side of the bed, and looked over at him, "Took you a long time tonight." It was more a statement than a question.

He replied in kind. "Yeah, couldn't think of anybody else."

Larry looked up and saw his town house in front of the car. He was parked in the driveway and he couldn't remember how long he had been there. He got out of the car and went inside, took one look at the place, and shuddered. Magazines and newspapers were strewn everywhere, as if a leaflet airdrop had been made by the enemy. Two jackets and a sweater he didn't recognize were hung haphazardly over chairs and brimming ash-trays crowded the mantlepiece, hearth and floor. Several tall bubble wine glasses containing a horrible bloodlike residue rested here and there on the dusty furniture, bearing mute testimony to his housekeeping abilities.

He inserted a tape in the deck and waded into the kitchen. One look and he almost threw up. It took him forty-five minutes to get a glimpse of the sink under the tidal wave of dirty dishes, but he was making headway. When he had the dishwasher loaded and running, he went back into the living room and piled everything that would move on the two sofas, then took the vacuum cleaner from the hall closet. Looking back into the jammed closet, he cringed and slammed the door.

He turned up the volume on the stereo to hear it above the choppy roar of the vacuum and began to pull the cleaner methodically back and forth across the carpeting. Three times the machine let out a noise like a wounded buffalo. Each time he upended it, he found a new treasure; one large gold earring (no idea whose), a black plastic champagne cork, and a single cuff link that would never fly again. When he shut off the machine to pry the battered cuff link out of the belt, he heard the doorbell above the sound of the music. Stepping to the stereo, he lowered the volume, then tripped over the vacuum cord as he made his way to the door. His next-door neighbor was standing on the stoop, wearing a very sexy dressing gown and a very grim expression.

"I like good music myself, friend, and 'Send in the Clowns' is one of my favorites, but I've about had it with the noise."

She pronounced the word about, *aboot,* with a definite

Canadian twang, but refined and hardly noticeable to all but a trained ear. Larry had a trained ear. "I'm sorry. I didn't realize I was disturbing the peace." He winced inwardly. It wasn't what he had wanted to say at all.

Close up, her hair was redder than he remembered it, a soft amber color like that of a summer sunset. She had pale, clear skin that looked extremely soft, and a figure that left Larry breathless. His gaze traveled down the folds of her silk gown, taking in the full breasts and narrow waist. He extended his hand, realized it held a vacuum cleaner attachment, and quickly shifted the long plastic nozzle to his other hand. "My name's Larry—"

"I don't care if it's Mantovani and you're conducting a Philharmonic rehearsal. Just turn it down a bit so I can get some sleep."

Larry glanced at his wristwatch to do something with the hand she refused to take. "It's four o'clock in the afternoon. You got to admit that's an odd time to be sleeping unless you're a cop or a hooker."

"With the traffic that goes through your place, I'm surprised you sleep at all." She paused and narrowed her eyes at him, maybe a little regretful for coming on so strong to a new neighbor. "Look, I've been up all night and I may be a little irritable. All I ask is that you keep it quiet, okay?"

She was damn near as tall as he was, and he stared almost directly into those large brown eyes, smiling like a kid on Christmas morning. "Why don't you come in and let me cook you breakfast. I think I've got an egg somewhere."

The tightness in her jaw softened a bit. "And if you don't, you'll lay one, right?"

Wild thoughts of being raped by a mad neighbor lady rushed through Larry's mind. "Come on, what do you have to lose?"

She shook her head. "Thank you anyway. It was Larry, wasn't it?"

"Yep. Larry DiaMonte. You've probably heard of me."

"Nope. I'm Lynn Singer. Does that mean anything to you?"

Larry shook his hed. "Should it?"

"*Captain* Lynn Singer, Los Angeles Police Department."

"You're a cop?"

She laughed and turned to go. "No, but if you keep waking me up, I'll join the force just to gain possession of a firearm."

She walked away, leaving Larry standing in the doorway with his mouth open.

52

FIVE

The next morning, Larry did two things when he got to the office. He handed Patte and Lew copies of an outline he had written the night before for the next episode of *Two Families,* an idea introducing a new character he was very excited about.

While they looked over the thin sheaf of papers with interest, he called a florist in Studio City. "That's right," he said into the phone. "I said *two* dozen white roses. No, no message on the card. Just sign it, From one of the clowns they sent in. Yeah, that's right, clowns."

He hung up and he was smiling as he swiveled his chair to face his two partners. Patte had finished reading the outline and Lew was scanning the last page. The girl nodded at him. "Not bad, my friend, not bad."

"Wasn't meant to be," Larry quipped back as he waited for Lew's reaction. Beckerman was the more conservative of the two, but he usually knew whereof he spoke.

He scratched his head and looked up at Larry. "Okay, let's see if I've got this straight." Lew always liked to think aloud. It helped him to better visualize the concept. "Karen decides she can't take Bob's machinations anymore and figures the only way she's gonna get rid of him is by selling her half of the duplex."

"Hey, the man can read," Patte grinned.

"Shut up, nitro." Larry turned to Lew. "Go ahead, glycerine."

Patte nodded and wrote down what Larry had just said as Lew muttered, "Yeah, I answered one of those ads, you know, about making big bucks by learning to read short paragraphs." Patte wrote that down too, and Larry shook his head as Lew continued. "So Karen hires this slick, high-pressure lady realtor who's a bit flakey—"

"A cross between Nixon and Lucretia Borga," Larry interjected.

"Yeah, right. And Bob, in his desperation, does everything in his power to queer the deal, not wanting to lose Karen again. Everything from moving the for sale sign to his half of the place after making it look like an earthquake just hit it, to hiring an actor to pose as a city inspector and condemn the property."

"That's about the size of it," Larry said.

"Don't you think the Claymore mines in the front yard is a bit much?" asked Lew.

"They're fake."

"Still . . ."

Larry got up and walked around his desk and perched on the edge of the long table. "Okay, it's got some holes in it. That's what they pay us an outrageous salary for, to make it work."

"This idea come from upstairs?" Patte asked.

"Nope."

Lew nodded his head like the wise old comedy writer he was. "Sounds a hell of a lot like your wife."

"So what?" Larry growled.

"Hey, don't bite my head off. I don't care if you want to parody Hermann Goering, as long as it's funny. I learned a long time ago you can't please all of the people none of the time." Lew smiled at Patte. "How come you're not writing that down, slick? That's a direct quote from Abe Lincoln."

"To Jefferson Davis, right?"

Larry relaxed a little and addressed them both. "You two kick it around. If it doesn't make all three of us at least snicker, then we'll shit-can it. Deal?"

Lew shrugged. "Why not?" Both men turned to Patte. "Pat?"

She began scribbling frantically on her pad. "I got an idea."

"See, what'd I tell you? You can always depend on Flash Gordon here," Larry admonished Lew.

"Yeah, if your name happens to be Dale Evans."

Patte spoke without looking up. "That's Arden, Dale Arden."

Larry laughed. "See what I mean?"

Larry took Sherman Way to Reseda Boulevard on the way home. It wasn't the most direct route, and it didn't help him avoid any afternoon traffic, but it did take him by his old house. Even if it was eight miles out of his way.

He didn't know what the hell he expected to see anyway. Sometimes he envisioned the house burned to the ground. But most of the time he longed for a glimpse of the kids playing football in the street, or maybe he'd see her again like he did one day last week. She'd been carrying a bag of groceries in from the car and she hadn't looked up as he sped by. She was wearing a new dress, one he hadn't seen before. He never liked her in green. Was she putting on a few pounds, or was it just his wishful thinking? If she got fat and ugly he knew he would feel better. He just wasn't sure why.

As he turned the corner he saw her car in the driveway with Lee Sanders's beige Jaguar sedan parked beside it. He slowed a little, fighting the mad urge to drive head on into both cars at sixty mph. As he passed the driveway he goosed the Porsche and the two-story ranch house shrunk away in his rearview mirror until it was out of sight.

When he pulled in at his place, his neighbor to the left, a twenty-two-year-old kid named Vince McCutchen, was rolling a shiny silver beer keg up his driveway. Larry drove into his garage and Vince hailed him as he got out of the car. "Hey, writer, how goes it?"

The kid was a USC student with a couple of sets of rich parents somewhere on the East Coast who were supporting him in a manner he was obviously enjoying. But he was a nice quiet kid, and Larry liked him, even though they had only exchanged a dozen words since Larry had moved in. "Gonna have a little nip before dinner?" Larry asked as he eyed the glistening keg.

Vince upended the keg and said, "That's just one of many. I'm throwing a masquerade party tonight." Vince had shoulder-length hair, a weak mustache, and a slight build. He looked very studious. "Why don't you drop by? Probably be about fifty or sixty people."

"What's the occasion?"

"Where you been, man? Halloween's in a few days."

"It is?" Larry was surprised. Then he felt lousy because he wouldn't be taking L.J. trick or treating this year. He shook his head and began walking away. "Thanks anyway, but I don't have a costume."

Vince ambled down to the end of his driveway and Larry stopped. "So what? There'll probably be a couple of dozen people who don't dress."

"That kind of party, huh?"

"You never can tell, " Vince smiled.

"I think I'd better pass."

"Hell, you might as well come. You won't be able to get any sleep anyway."

"Well, maybe I'll drop by for a drink. Let me see how

things go." Larry looked up at Lynn Singer's place. There was no sign of life. He wondered if she had received the roses. "Say, have you seen the lady that drives the blue BMW today?"

Vince shook his head. "You mean the ice lady?"

"Huh?"

"I've said hello to her a couple of times. She's either deaf or don't speak English. She keeps some weird hours, man. I see her going out dressed like a queen in evening gowns and furs, and coming home by herself at four or five in the morning."

"What are you doing up at that hour, jogging?"

"I got insomnia."

"Yeah, I saw your insomnia the other day. Does she have a friend?"

"Me," Vince grinned.

"Thanks. See you later."

Larry went inside and cooked dinner; something that came out of the freezer and went through the microwave oven in six minutes. It might have been macaroni and cheese, he thought, as he pushed it around his plate with the fork. Or sawdust and cardboard.

He left the plate on the counter, mixed himself a gin and tonic, and went out to the patio. He sat in one of the yellow director chairs next to the fence that separated his yard from Lynn's. He sat there sipping the drink and watched the sun go down, listening for any sign of life from next door. Maybe she wasn't coming home tonight. She probably had a dinner date, anyway.

He finished the drink and went upstairs. Undressing, he stood in front of the full-length mirrors that covered the closet doors in the master suite and studied his body. No fat, fairly wide shoulders, and pretty good muscle tone. Hell, he looked thirty. Why not go to the party?

He showered and toweled himself dry under the

bathroom sunlamp. Then he trimmed his beard and used the dryer on his unruly hair.

When he was finished in the bathroom he went to the closet and put on a red silk shirt, black slacks, and black leather boots. He threaded a black leather belt with a U.S. Cavalry insignia on the buckle through the loops of his pants and pulled a black vest over the shirt.

Standing back in front of the mirrors to get a full-length view, he admired himself. It wasn't much, but it was as close to a costume as he was likely to come. He could always say he was Sam Houston. Hell, he looked more like John Huston.

As he left his town house, he looked over to see if there were any lights next door. Her place was dark and he shrugged as he made his way between the twenty or so cars that fronted Vince's unit.

The girl that opened the door was a pink cat. She wore a body stocking, fluffy white ears, and a long straight tail that she held in one hand. Black whiskers were painted on her cheeks, and large black letters saying "A little kitten never hurt anybody" ran across her full breasts.

He looked at the packed living room over her shoulder and the cloud of cannabis smoke that wafted out of the entry hall almost gagged him. "Yes?" she said, as if she thought he had the wrong address.

"I'm, ah, Vince's friend." He almost said grandfather. The kitten couldn't have been more than nineteen, and from the look of the rest of the group, that was probably the median age.

"Hey, writer, come on in!" Vince moved out of the crowd and put his arm around the kitten's waist. "Glad you could make it. Larry, this is Anita. Honey, this is Larry DiMonte, my neighbor."

Larry nodded at Anita, and then said to Vince, "I just stopped by to tell you you're not making enough noise. I almost dozed off twice."

Vince chuckled and drew him into the room, closing the door. He was wearing a full dress Waffen SS uniform, replete with Iron Cross and monocle. "Who you supposed to be?" Anita asked, and Larry could see that she was more than slightly stoned.

"William Goldman."

"Who?"

Vince laughed and grabbed Larry by the shoulder. "There's anything you want to drink on the patio, the kitchen is loaded with food, and there's plenty of grass floating around. Just make yourself at home."

Larry nodded and elbowed his way through the packed bodies, feeling like an octogenarian at a nursery school. A slightly built pirate was standing at the end of a long table that had been set up on the patio, and he smiled at Larry as the older man stepped through the open doorway and poured Scotch into a paper cup. "Hi, I'm Chris."

Larry introduced himself and the two stood exchanging pleasantries as Larry looked back into the main room at the people sprawled on the floor. There were several girls dressed as Playboy bunnies, a hunchback of indeterminate sex, a smattering of surgeons, and the cowboys outnumbered the Indians about three to one. Great. He was the only one over twenty-three, and he squirmed as he watched the glances he was getting. In self-defense he kept up the conversation with the pirate.

After a few minutes of small talk he was forced to admit what he did for a living. The pirate winked with his good eye. "No kiddin'? I watch that show every Thursday night. It's my favorite."

Larry didn't have the heart to tell Short John Silver that *Two Families* was a Monday night prime time show. He just poured another double ration of Scotch into his cup and excused himself.

Going back into the living room, he found a bare spot in a corner and leaned against the wall, trying to figure out just what the hell he was doing here. "Want a toke?" He jumped at the sound of the voice beside him, turned, and was confronted by a girl whose face was painted in a pattern of black and white checkers, the design matching her dress—what there was of it. She looked like a Kiss album cover.

She held out a joint and Larry just stared at it stupidly. He was from the old school, and he never even took aspirin unless it was absolutely necessary. He used to tell his friends at parties that maybe he'd try drugs some day, whenever he came down off his natural high. Well, maybe he had just come down, he admitted, as he reached for the joint. "How do I do it?"

Her large brown eyes widened. "You're putting me on."

He had been around enough pot smokers to know the drill, but he was enjoying himself. "Nope, you're looking at a virgin."

She took a long pull and inhaled twice, sharply, then held the smoke in her lungs as long as she could. He followed her lead and sucked in the foul smelling smoke. They finished the number together in silence and she moved off, leaving him staring blankly at the opposite wall.

Half an hour later Larry was sitting in the center of a small group near the fireplace, waving his hands and telling war stories about the making of a hit TV show. He was high and he sucked on a purple bong that was being passed around the circle. For the first time in longer than he cared to remember he felt no pain. He was on, he had an attentive audience, and even if they were just patronizing an old man, he didn't give a shit.

"No, no, no, you don't understand. TV *is* an imitative

medium. If a show is a hit, everybody and his dog is rushing to duplicate the magic formula. I wouldn't be surprised if we have two new shows next season, one called *Mork* and the other called *Mindy,*" he said to a raven-haired Vampira that sat cross-legged to his right. She wore a red one-piece bathing suit that plunged so deeply he could make out her pubic hair.

"I only watch PBS," Vampira remarked offhandedly. When she opened her mouth Larry was confronted by a set of braces that contained enough track to run the B & O Railroad. He winced at the glare from her mouth and shouted above the noise of the hard rock music to be heard. "You know what you like and you do what you want, right?" he leered.

She smiled back at him. "That's right. I'm a free spirit."

Larry leaned over and cupped a hand to her ear as he whispered, "If you're as free a spirit as you claim to be, you'll put down your drink, pick up your purse, and we'll walk out of here together."

She didn't bat an eye at the proposition, just placed her glass on the hearth and stood with her purse in her hands. smiled and rose, taking her hand and pulling her along through the press of people as he ran interference across the center of the room. Life was getting better. All of a sudden things were beginning to look up.

Vince was sitting on the hall step engaged in animated conversation with a girl in a gypsy outfit. Larry laughed aloud at the sight of the incongrous couple as he side-stepped between them. Vince looked up and gave him a sly grin. Larry nodded back and pulled Vampira to the door.

He opened it to see Lynn Singer standing there on the front stoop with her finger poised over the bell button. She was more formally dressed than their last encounter: wine blouse and lavender riding skirt, and tall brown boots. She was wearing large glasses that gave her the appearance of a puckish, very attractive owl. It didn't take an IQ of two hundred to see that she was pissed.

She began to speak before he could open his mouth. "Somebody's blocking my driveway, and I'd like the car moved before I have it towed—oh, it's you. Somehow, I should have known."

"I, ah . . ." Larry was unable to complete his greeting because he had absolutely no idea what to say.

Vince rose and waved at Lynn. "Come on in and join the party."

"I don't want any trouble. I just want the green MG moved. Now."

The authority in her voice angered Vince. "Well, the hell with you, broad!"

Larry let go of Vampira's hand and found his voice. "She's a cop, Vince."

"Ah, yeah." Vince paled and raised his voice to the crowd. "Whoever owns the green MG best move it."

"It's mine," Vampira said, as she brushed past Lynn and headed down the walkway. Lynn pivoted on her heel and followed. Larry slammed the door behind him and caught up with her halfway to the street, grabbing her arm.

"Wait a minute. At least let me explain."

She removed his hand from her arm with a grip so strong it surprised him. "I said I didn't want any trouble. Now, you just go back to your party, and I'll go home."

The MG's engine started and Vampira backed the little car out of Lynn's driveway into the street. Braces gleaming in the glare from the streetlight, she waved a bare arm in Larry's direction and laid a strip of rubber halfway down the block as she accelerated away. Larry frowned. That, too, figured.

Lynn was moving now and Larry stepped up his pace to keep abreast of her. "Did you, ah, get the flowers?"

She stopped so fast he almost tripped over her. "You sent those?"

He couldn't tell if she were pleased or angry. "Sure. Didn't you read the card?"

"I did, but I don't know any clones."

"Clones? It was *clowns!* I'll kill 'em! I'll go to the flower shop first thing in the morning and with my bare hands I'll personally strangle the illiterate responsible. And no jury in the world would convict me."

"Don't bet on it," she stated, and then, "They were very nice. And totally unnecessary."

He took her arm again. "Let's go for a walk. It's a fantastic night and I'd like to talk to you."

She didn't resist his grip this time. "About what?"

"I haven't got the faintest idea. Give me a minute and I'm sure I'll come up with something."

This time she actually laughed. It was the most melodious sound he had never heard. "Goodnight, Mr.—"

"Larry DiaMonte. Is it Miss, Mrs., or Mizz?"

"I would hope it's Mr., unless you're awfully versatile with your wardrobe."

Larry groaned. "That's good. But it still doesn't tell me what to call you."

"I told you, you can call me Captain."

"Midnight, Marvel, or Ahab?"

"Bligh," she growled playfully and Larry's heart almost stopped.

"Look, I want to apologize for what happened yesterday. I'm really a proctologist from Nyack, New Jersey, staying here with my twin brother for a couple of weeks. My brother explained the misunderstanding and since he's such a pill, I figured I should say I'm sorry for the both of us."

"And if I buy that, you have some beachfront property in Bakersfield to show me, right?"

Larry increased the pressure on her arm and steered her out of the driveway and down the street, under the newly planted trees. At least she had a sense of humor.

"Naw, I'm not into real estate anymore," he grunted. He doubted if she'd appreciate the humor in that remark, so he refrained from explaining it. They walked in silence for a few hundred feet. She didn't attempt to remove her arm from his grip, nor did she move in any closer. His mind raced furiously for a topic they could both discuss that would keep her with him as long as possible. "You're in bunko, right?"

"Homicide."

"Like in death?"

She turned slightly and looked in his eyes. "It's a living."

Larry chuckled. He was really beginning to like her. If he could figure a way to get her into bed tonight, he'd be in love. "Funny, you don't look homicidal."

"Oh, I don't know. I came pretty close when your bloody stereo was driving me up the wall."

"You ever have to, ah . . ." he stammered, trying vainly to decide if she were wearing a gun on her hip or carrying it in her purse.

"Never in the line of duty. You get most of that working nightside vice."

Larry blushed, wondering if she could tell in the semidarkness. "No, I, ah, meant, have you had to shoot anybody, I mean, with your gun?"

"Not yet, but the night's young." She smiled, with a look of bland innocence in her eyes.

They sat on a bench at the edge of a patch of greenery at the end of the street. Larry placed his arm behind her on the rough wood and faced her profile. "Now that I've got you cornered, you're doomed to hear my life story. You know that, don't you?"

She tilted her head back slightly and he studied the

curve of her throat as she looked up at the stars.

"You're a comedy writer, recently separated, a little absent-minded, somewhat sentimental, continually on the make, and right now—" she turned her head to peer into his eyes— "a bit stoned."

"How the hell did you know all that?"

"What do I do for a living, friend?"

"Come on now, admit it, you made some discreet inquiries because you were interested, right?"

"I should have added conceited to that list. No, just a matter of simple deduction, Watson. Your license plate is a dead giveaway to your profession. A double entendre, but not too hard to figure out." She pointed at his right hand. "You're wearing that ring on the wrong hand. You fidget with it while you talk, as if you're not used to it there. You forget about other people's feelings. Witness the loudness of your sound system, which by the way, is quite good. The roses prove you're sentimental, and your eyes and manner make it fortunate for both of us that I'm not a nark."

"You left out 'constantly on the make.'"

"I have a feeling that subject is going to surface quite soon enough."

Larry took another tack, avoiding a response he wanted desperately to make. "You wouldn't really arrest me, would you?"

"Mr. DiaMonte, I would arrest my doddering gray-haired mother were she in violation of the law. With a tear in my eye, of course, but with a dedication to duty that you wouldn't believe."

Larry looked at the gleam in her eye and decided he was being stroked by an expert. "You're not really a cop, are you?"

"Worse than that, I'm not even a commissioned officer."

"What are you then?"

Lynn rose and straightened her skirt, a purely feminine gesture that caused Larry to lean forward and bring his knees together to keep his rising erection in check.

"I have no desire to discuss my personal life with a relative stranger, Mr. DiaMonte," she stated formally.

Larry jumped up, slowly, and said, "Look, come on over for a brandy at least. I promise I'll keep the music on low this time."

"I bet you would." She nodded. He was completely destroyed by her abrupt departure, but there was no way he could keep her there short of wrestling her to the ground and dragging her into his place by the hair. A tactic that, he felt, would leave him minus several fingers and maybe even a foot.

She walked away, leaving him standing open-mouthed, stopped in a moment of indecision that almost gave him religion, and said, "Maybe another time." She smiled. "When you're a little more sentimental and a little less on the make."

SIX

Larry went inside and looked at the wall clock in the kitchen. Eleven thirty. Too early to go to bed and too late to call anybody. He could go back to the party. The thought made him wince. Or he could go for a drive. Might as well have a drink first, though.

He stiffled a strong urge to turn the stereo volume up full as he inserted an old Simon and Garfunkel tape into the deck. He mixed a drink as he listened to "Homeward Bound." Dammit! He hated to be alone. Especially late at night. He couldn't understand the strange feeling of loneliness. Many a night after the kids were in bed and Robyn was out on a presentation, he had sat with his drink and listened to music or watched the *Tomorrow Show,* and he hadn't felt alone. Now he was free, high, and twenty-one, and goddamn if he should feel so fucking lost.

He stared at the painting for a while, getting angrier, then walked to the desk and plopped down in the chair with his feet propped on its top. He reached for the phone and punched Branda's number. If nothing else, she would at least be company. Whatever gets you through the night, DiaMonte.

He let the phone ring fifteen times before he replaced the receiver. Okay, you can't expect her to stay home waiting for your call, dummy. He went back to the bar and poured another Scotch. If only the doorbell would ring and Lynn would be standing there in a negligee with a bottle of wine and an inviting expression. He fantasized about that for a while, then gave it up, suddenly unable to visualize being in bed with her. Face it, ole buddy, the lady intimidates you. She's got her shit together, and the last thing she needs is a relationship with a loser.

More and more lately, he found himself thinking in those terms. He came from an old-line Italian family where divorce had been a dirty word. Even though he considered himself a modern, sophisticated man, he hated to be a failure at anything. And he had certainly been less than successful at marriage. If he only knew the answer. How could a woman he had loved for years, someone he had faith and trust in, a person that was an integral part of his daily life and personality, how could she just turn him off like a light switch?

And for some creepy little bastard with no hair, yet. He didn't know who he hated more, Robyn, her boyfriend, or himself. Sure, it's your fault, you asshole. You never sent *her* two dozen roses. Ole Baldy probably sent her a single posey and won her heart—among other things.

He went back to the phone and began to thumb through his new address book. He hadn't met many girls lately, but there were a few names scribbled in black felt-tipped pen on the white pages. Nobody he dared call at this hour, though. It was coming up on one AM. He was surprised at the passage of time as he glanced at the clock again. The last thing he needed was to look like a fool.

When he got to the G's, he saw Patte Gordon's home number. A friend in need, huh? Why the hell not?

She answered on the first ring, which surprised him. He didn't even have time to prepare a snappy delivery line in answer to her wide awake hello.

"Hi, Flash, did I get you up?"

"No." It was a simple answer and he wasn't sure she knew who it was.

"It's me, Larry."

"You're drunk."

"Semi-inebriated. Are you busy?"

"I'm not alone."

"Oh."

There was a long silence. "Are you all right?" The concern in her voice was evident to him. He had never called her at home before except on business, and he must have shocked the hell out of her.

"Yeah, I'm fine. Just wanted to rap with somebody. It's okay, I'll talk to you tomorrow."

"What's wrong?"

"Wrong? Nothing's wrong. I've got this leggy blonde over here and we were arguing about who played opposite Robert Montgomery in *Night Must Fall*."

"Rosalind Russell. In the English film of the same name, it was Albert Finney and Mona Washburne."

"I knew you could set the record straight."

"Who'd you think it was?"

"Jill St. John, with Hermione Gingold in the British version. Goodnight, Flash."

Before he could hang up, she said, "It shouldn't take you less than twenty minutes to get here. By that time I'll be alone and decent."

"Wait a min—"

"Just get in that expensive car of yours and drive. I'm putting the coffee on now."

There was a *click* and Larry was holding a dead phone. Hmmmm, a friend in need, indeed.

Patricia Ann Gordon lived in a high-rise apartment

building in Van Nuys. The traffic had been extremely heavy for the hour and it wasn't until thirty minutes later that Larry stood ringing the bell of her sixth-floor apartment. The door opened and Patte smiled up at him. She was wearing a bulky blue robe that made her look like a fifteenth century monk. Her hair was fluffy, as if she had just washed and toweled it dry, and Larry could see a trace of dampness on her throat and forehead. "You happen to have a kick stool and some rope?" he asked, as she moved aside to let him enter.

"That bad, huh?"

"Badder," he said as she closed the door. The interior of the apartment was decorated with movie stills and posters that covered most of the available wall space and parts of the ceiling. Above the sofa on the far wall, a Picasso print was sandwiched between a *Bad News Bears* poster and a double truck *Roller Boogie* ad cut out of an old *Variety.* The print looked out of place: a blue man, woman and child standing on a blue beach in front of blue water under a blue sky.

Must have been his blue period, Larry decided as he fell heavily to the sofa and put his feet atop a pile of magazines that spilled off the long glass coffee table and wound across the cluttered floor. In one corner near the balcony doors, pages of script were loosely strewn in a wide semicircle. Larry nodded at the homework. "Going over the Christmas two-parter?"

"I was earlier."

"Are you acquainted with the Soviet nuclear capability?" Larry asked abruptly.

"No, but if you'll hum the first few bars, I'll try to sing along," she replied, as she perched on the arm of the sofa.

Larry made a face at her. "Very funny. Old, but still marginally humorous. Do you realize that tomorrow morning the world may be a pile of radioactive ash?"

"Is that the beginnings of a proposition?" Her eyebrows rose as if she were insulted.

Larry looked shocked. "Ah, no. Hell no." She pouted and he couldn't tell if she was really disappointed, or just faking it. "I just needed to talk to somebody."

Patte nodded. "I can understand that. I was divorced once myself."

"*You* were married?"

"Well, shit, fella," she replied indignantly. "I had to get married."

"You did?"

"Yeah, very few single people qualify for a divorce under California law. But it's okay now that I'm a member of D.A."

"D.A.?" It was too late. Larry had walked right into it.

"Divorcees Anonymous. When you feel the desire to remarry, they send over a potbellied bald guy with a six-pack, and he grumbles and watches football all day."

Larry laughed. "Hey, that's good. Did you write it down?"

She pointed to the script on the floor. "It's part of the show."

Larry winked at her. "I thought I heard it somewhere before."

"I only steal from the best sources."

He made a gun of his hand and fired a finger at her. "Touche."

"Anyway, why is that so hard to believe?" she asked seriously.

"Oh, I dunno. I guess I just never pictured you married. Want to tell me about it?"

"No."

"Good. I don't need to hear your troubles. I'm here to tell you mine."

"No shit?"

71

"You figured that out, huh? Got any Scotch?"

Patte rose and opened a cabinet door above the kitchen alcove, fumbling around inside. "Got some Old Bushjacket."

"Christ! Okay, anything'll do in a pinch."

Her hand came out of the cabinet clutching the neck of a Chevas Regal bottle. She waved it at him. "Or this?"

"All right! Why didn't you say that in the first place?"

She cocked her head to one side and grimaced. "'Cause I don't know I got to show you my Chevaz Regal, mon," she said in a Cockney accent.

He laughed far more than the routine deserved and watched her as she poured the amber liquid into a heavy crystal glass. She was cute, in a doll-like sort of way, like somebody had scrubbed her skin with Ivory soap for about twenty years. She had deep blue eyes, made more intense by the contacts she wore. He knew she hated glasses, and he had only seen her wearing them once, the day he had hired her.

She had been an aspiring writer with no experience, and she had submitted serveral story ideas on different occasions, managing to get a foot in his door through a friend in administration. And although her work showed some merit, Larry made it a hard and firm rule to work only with established writers. Not necessarily the most talented, he had found out the hard way, but people he knew he could rely upon when the gunfire started and the shrapnel was as thick as falling snow.

The last time he had tried to ease her gently out of his office with a smile and a pat on the back, she had stopped him with an icy stare. "You're a pompous bastard, you know that?" she had told him, very calmly. He hadn't known whether to take offense or laugh. Nobody had ever called him that before, although he had been referred to by many other descriptive adjectives. "How the hell do you know I can't do the job unless you give me a chance? I've just about had it with this Catch 44 bullshit! You look at my stuff and you say it's good! It *is* good! Just because my only experience is writing PR copy for a Med-evac unit doesn't mean I'm not good at what I do. For God's sake, you can always fire me tomorrow!"

"Give me one reason why I should hire you today," he had asked.

"I'm Jewish and you're Italian. Together we can control the industry."

Well, he hadn't fired her tomorrow, or the next day for that matter. She handed him the drink and tucked her legs under her as she sat on the floor beside the couch. She wasn't really hard to look at, he admitted, and suddenly he was envying the guy that had been occupying her bed that night. Here was a nice lady that shared all his interests and his twisted sense of humor. Better off he probably couldn't be. "I keep having this recurrring nightmare— when I sleep at all," Larry said after taking a healthy swig of his drink.

"Tell me about it."

"It's crazy. I'm in this casino restaurant in Vegas with Robyn and another couple. I don't know who they are, other than they're trade people, because we're talking business. Robyn and I are happily married—everything's nice—we're even playing kneeses under the table. Then she excuses herself to go to the restroom. She doesn't come back, and I begin to get concerned, but I don't want to show it. Then this guy gets up and leaves, and I'm sitting there talking to his date, or rather, listening to her, because all she can talk about is how she's going to break into show biz."

Larry paused and handed Patte his empty glass. She rose and refilled it. "Go on, I'm listening."

"I told you it was nutty. Pretty soon I'm in a real panic

because neither Robyn nor this handsome dude is coming back. I get up to go look for them and this girl just goes on talking, like I was still sitting across from her."

"Sounds like real life," Patte interjected, without smiling.

"Yeah. Anyway, I find myself walking through this big casino. All the slots are going full tilt. It's noisy, bright. Now the insane part. I'm wearing a three-piece dark business suit and tie, and I look down and I'm in my bare feet. No socks or shoes, I can't find Robyn or this guy, and everybody's looking at my feet and cracking up. That's when I wake up in a cold sweat."

"A classic, textbook case," Patte remarked professionally.

"Well, I'm sure glad somebody understands it," Larry said sarcastically. "Care to explain it to a layman, Herr Doktor?"

"Sure, it's simple. When you fall asleep you toss the covers off and your feet get cold. The nightmare stems from a deep-rooted desire to keep your tootsies warm. Take two ski socks and call me in the morning."

"You're a big help," Larry sighed.

"Is that what you really want?"

"What?"

"Help."

Larry considered her question for a moment. "I vant to be cured! I vant to play zee harpsicord again!"

Patte didn't laugh, she just stared at him. "You're standing in the center of a Vegas casino because you don't do anything on a small scale," she said evenly. "And you're in your bare feet with everybody pointing and laughing while your wife's out making it with another man. Doesn't that tell you something?"

Larry shook his head, afraid to speak. Patte went on, "Instead of wearing horns, you're shoeless in front of God and the whole world. The object of great embarrassment. Don't take no hundred dollar an hour shrink to figure that one out."

Larry frowned. "You think so?"

"Hell, yes! You think of yourself as being cuckolded, and being the egotist you are, you find yourself in the midst of the busiest, brightest place this side of the Beverly Hilltops."

"How the hell would you know that?"

Patte brought her legs out from under her body and extended her bare feet toward him. "Because, fella, I've been there myself."

Larry placed his glass on the coffee table and stood. Reaching down he took both her hands and pulled her to her feet. "You know what I need more than anything right now?"

"I'm afraid to ask." Her voice was low and he could see the nervousness in her smile.

"I need a hug from a friend." He grinned. She came into his arms, locking her hands behind his back and squeezing with all her might. Her head rested in the crook of his neck. She tilted back slightly, brushing his cheek with her hair. He had never held her before and he was surprised at how good she felt. She was smaller than Robyn, lighter, and she seemed to fit the contours of his body perfectly.

He squeezed back, and they stood there for a moment holding on to each other as if they would both fall off the world if they let go. She smelled clean and fresh. No perfume, just a crisp outdoor odor that was beginning to turn him on. He pulled back a little and placed one hand under her chin, raising it so he could look at her. She stared into his eyes briefly, then closed hers, parting her lips just enough so he could see the pinkness of her tongue. He kissed her softly. She responded eagerly, pressing hard against him.

75

When he removed his lips from hers he felt a dampness on his cheek. There were two tiny tears on her face. "Hey, what's that all about?" he asked, as he touched the wetness with a fingertip.

"I hurt for you," she said softly.

He grabbed her and held her close, her head resting on his shoulder. "You know what they say about that, don't you?"

"No, but I'm afraid you're going to tell me."

"They say that if somebody else's tears touch your skin, they leave indelible marks." As he spoke, he was staring at the *Bad News Bears* poster behind her, looking at the kids in their baseball uniforms. "I never see my kids anymore, you know that?" It didn't even sound like his voice. It was gravelly and low. "I can't face them. I can't look into their eyes, Pat. Ever since Steve was born, I've looked forward to teaching him how to drive, helping him pick out his first car. Now somebody else is going to do that, and all the other things I planned to do. She took my kids away from me and I'll never forgive her for that."

Her hair was moist against his cheek. How was that possible? Then he knew as she reached up and touched his wet face with her hand. He was crying now. Jesus, how low the mighty have fallen.

She must have read his mind. "It's all right."

He enveloped her in a bear hug because he didn't want to look into those knowing eyes. Then he began to sob uncontrollably. Terrific. Here I am, a forty-year-old man, standing in the middle of a room with a girl I hardly know emotionally, and I'm crying like a baby. "I'm sorry I called you a crunt," he said when he regained his composure.

She laughed the old Flash Gordon laugh and held him at arm's length, her eyes twinkling. "You were wrong, you know."

"I know."

"I use Pepsodent, not Colgate."

That broke the tension and they both fell to the sofa laughing. When Larry was able to control himself again, he said, "You're fantastic, Flash."

"Hell, I could have told you that. Matter of fact, I think I have a time or two."

Larry suddenly wanted to make love to her. But then, Larry wanted to make love to everybody. It was his way of proving that he was still a man, even though his wife had dumped him. His way of covering his bare feet. Question was, did Pat? She looked and acted as if she did. He could just come right out and ask her. What the hell could it hurt?"

"I gotta go now," he said involuntarily. Their friendship was what could suffer.

"If you want to spend what's left of the night . . ." Her voice trailed off and it looked to him as if it were difficult for her to mouth the words.

"I want to, but I'm not."

"Promise me one thing?"

"You got it."

"If you get to feeling lousy again, call me?"

"Believe it." He leaned down and kissed her gently on the forehead. Then he walked to the door and without looking back, closed it behind him.

Patricia Ann Gordon sat staring at the door for a long time. Then she finally said, "Shit."

PART TWO

The Headless Horseman of Hollywood

SEVEN

It was Monday night and Larry sat on his sofa going over a script. The TV set was on and he was taping tonight's *Two Families* on his video recorder. He watched the lead opposition show absent-mindedly, getting up every ten minutes to switch to the third network.

He had been celibate for the last three weeks, out of choice, he assured himself daily, since he was up to his nostrils in work. Branda had gone to Cabo San Lucas with somebody or other, and for reasons he was unable to fathom he was beginning to miss her.

He had caught fleeting glimpses of Lynn Singer half a dozen times, but never had a chance to speak to her. He had even tacked a note to her door asking her to call him, but she hadn't responded. Vince had been right, she sure did keep weird hours. If she wasn't a cop, she should have been.

As a writer he should be able to come up with some brilliant plan that would shuffle her into his arms, like starting the place afire so he could rescue her in the middle of the night. Hmmmm, not a bad idea for the show, he thought, as he made a note on the script margin.

He still had strong hopes he'd run into her by accident and she'd fall into his arms in a swoon. He figured the odds were also pretty good she'd seek him out. Maybe two or three thousand to one.

He had phoned Benny Frankel's office daily for the last week, but the producer hadn't returned his calls. His secretary had given him a new excuse every time he called, and he was beginning to get a little pissed off. The lack of contact was either a good sign or a bad sign. Frankel was too busy getting financing for *Five'll Get You Ten* and lining up a packaging deal, or he didn't have the heart to tell Larry that the project had about as much chance of being sold as a musical comedy about the Ayatollah Khomeini written, directed, and narrated by the ex-Shah.

He saw Patte Gordon every day. Neither had made any mention of their brief encounter. She was her old bubbly self and only when he looked half dead did she ask how he was. She and Lew had cranked out a first draft for the episode about the lady realtor, and it was good. Larry had spent a great deal of time polishing it, then submitted it upstairs. It went through the usual channels like a bobsled on new ice, and it had been taped last week for airing on the next Monday night. He felt like phoning Robyn and telling her to make sure she didn't miss it, but that would be too much like gloating. Maybe he'd just drop her a note.

He had avoided his son's soccer games, and he was feeling a little better about the whole situation, not having seen Robyn. He missed the kids, but he figured if they wanted to see him badly enough they could always pick up the phone. Every day when he got home he rushed to the answering machine and waded through the messages and hangups, hoping he'd hear Steve's voice. He worried about his oldest son the most. The boy was at a delicate enough age without complicating his life with a messy divorce. He had always been a quiet, reserved kid, and

Larry never knew what he was really thinking. It was difficult to talk to Steve, and sometimes Larry felt ther was no basis for communication at all.

The Munchkin was a different story. He'd make it if he were cast adrift on an inner tube in the middle of the Pacific with a penknife and a box of Pop-Tarts. The little guy was a fighter and he seldom let adversity get the best of him. He was a lot like Larry had been as a child. Would have been nice if Larry had been able to carry that attitude over into adulthood.

Larry grimaced and leaned forward on the edge of the sofa rubbing his back. Every once in a while he'd do something stupid and throw a vertebra out, and it was beginning to feel like one of those time. That was all he needed now. He was about five days behind, and he doubted if he would ever see daylight again. "That's what abstinence does for you, old man," he said aloud. "Makes the hip grow tender."

He got up to go to the bathroom but never made it. The pain was like a knife blade in his side, and he blanched and grabbed at his back, letting out a loud groan. "Ohhhh, shit!"

God was finally getting him for past transgressions, but wow! Talk about overkill! He hobbled to the bar and crouched as he splashed some brandy into a glass. He gulped the liquor and started coughing. He had experienced back pains before, but never like this. He slid to the floor in a fetal position, white fingers gripping the glass and shaking so badly he spilled the booze on his pants. He was frightened. Maybe the pain would go away in a few minutes. Sure, it was just a cramp brought on by overwork and mental stress. No problem, just bite the bullet and ride it out.

Ten minutes later the pain abated and he managed a weak smile. Then it hit him again like a runaway train. He tried taking deep breaths and expelling them through his mouth, but that didn't seem to do much good. He stared longingly at the telephone, wondering if he should call an ambulance. The pain was getting worse and he was afraid he was going to lose consciousness. He was dizzy and nauseous, but he pulled himself to his feet with a great effort and began to sway toward the garage. He went out the kitchen door, thumbed the switch that opened the garage door, then fell against the car. He knew he'd never be able to drive himself, as he went to his knees and pressed his forehead against the cold metal of the hood. "If you fall down every few feet, DiaMonte, it's really gonna cut your time to the Coast."

He moaned again as he came to his feet, bracing his body on the side of the car and sliding down to the open garage door. The BMW was in the next driveway and he stumbled around it and limped up the walkway, letting out a *whoosh* of relief as he leaned against Lynn's doorbell. She opened the door. She was wearing street clothes, as if she had just come in. "I hate to bother you," Larry gasped, "but I think I'm dying."

Lynn shook her head. "And you want me to give you mouth to mouth resus—" She hesitated, as she took in his chalk-white features and perspiration-stained shirt. "What's wrong?"

"I, ah, bad back pain, feels like I've been shot. Figured I'd check with you first."

She took his arm and supported his weight on her shoulder, closing the door behind her. "Come on, I'll drive you to the hospital."

"I would really appreciate that."

Larry almost passed out twice on the way to the hospital. He reached over and took Lynn's right hand whenever a particularly bad spasm hit and squeezed hard. He was holding on tightly when they pulled up in front of the hospital emergency entrance fifteen minutes later.

"—Don't think I can walk," Larry said after trying to straighten up in the car seat.

"You stay put. I'll get a wheelchair and some help." She was back in seconds with the chair and an orderly. They helped Larry into the chair and wheeled him through the electric doors to the lobby. Lynn conversed briefly with the duty nurse, then Larry was whisked into a curtained alcove beyond a set of large green doors. He lay there on a gurney for almost half an hour listening to an intern in the next alcove dress a man's cut finger. That figures, he groaned, somebody has a hangnail treated while I expire.

Finally after what seemed like days, a tall nurse with a friendly smile bustled in with a clipboard to take Larry's insurance information and case history. "The lady that brought me in," he managed to grunt between seizures, "is she still here?"

"She's waiting in the lobby," the nurse said as she scribbled professionally on a form.

"I want her in here with me."

"Is she your wife?"

"No, she's a police officer. I'm under arrest and she's not supposed to leave my side."

"I'm sorry. Maybe she can come in after the doctor has seen you."

"They busted me for—oh shit!" He hunched up into a ball and clenched his teeth to keep from screaming. "For aggravated assault and multiple rape. Better get her in here before I get the urge again."

The nurse made a hasty exit and in less than a minute Lynn was beside Larry's gurney. As soon as he saw her he grabbed her hand and held on for dear life. "What did you tell that poor nurse?"

Larry managed a weak smile. "I told her that we were Siamese twins and I was suffering massive pain because we were no longer joined at the belly." Lynn shook her head and Larry held on tight until the doctor arrived. The intern didn't look much older than Steve, but he had an air of confidence about him that must have been standard issue in med school.

"What the hell is it, Doc? I feel like I've been kicked by a horse."

The doctor pressed his fingers into Larry's side and Larry almost passed out again. "You ever have a kidney stone before?"

"Hell no."

"Well, we'll have to run an IVP on you, but I think you may have one now." The doctor took a syringe from the nurse's sterile tray and began to prepare Larry's hip for the injection. "I'm going to give you something to alleviate the pain. You should be feeling better in a few minutes." Larry hated needles, but it looked as if he had little choice this time.

The nurse was completing the forms as the doctor readied the injection. "How old are you, Mr. DiaMonte?"

"Ah—"

"Forty," Lynn told her.

"How the hell did you know that? Ouch!" The needle went in and stayed there for about six hours. Lynn leaned down and stroked his forehead.

"We going to get into the deductive process again, huh?"

"Hey, I'm feeling better already," Larry sighed as the doctor removed the needle.

"We'll be admitting him to the hospital, miss," the doctor said to Lynn. "He should spend a peaceful night and you can see him in the morning."

The doctor and nurse left and Lynn said, "Is there

anyone I can call for you?"

Larry thought about that for a moment. He should have Lynn call Robyn and tell her he was dying. She'd rush to his side in his hour of need, clutch his withered head to her breast and weep tears of repentance, assuring him that she'd be with him to the end.

Or she would inquire coolly if he had changed beneficiaries on his life insurance policy.

"No, I'll call my office in the morning and they can take care of everything." The drug was taking effect and he was beginning to feel drowsy. "Why don't you spend the night here keeping vigil beside my sickbed? Then, when I wake up i the morning the first thing I'll see is your beautiful face. Or better yet, maybe I can get them to give me a double bed." He figured if he insulted her delicate sensibilities he could always blame it on the medication.

"I have a feeling you'll pull through without me. I am concerned about the nurses, though."

He laughed and squeezed her hand. The pain was almost gone now. "Thanks," he said sincerely. "I really appreciate what you did."

She placed her hand on his forehead, like a mother checking her child for fever. "You take care of yourself." Then she removed a piece of note paper from her purse and wrote something on it. She kissed him on the cheek as she stuffed the paper into his shirt pocket. "That's my phone number. Call me if you need anything."

She walked away and Larry lay there smiling. Maybe kidney stones weren't so bad after all.

EIGHT

Larry hated hospitals. He had good reason to. When he was six years old he had cut his foot on a jagged piece of glass concealed by a puddle he had been playing in. It was a bad gash and they had to operate to repair the tendon, which necessitated a hospital stay of several days. On the afternoon he was scheduled to be discharged, he came down with a bad sore throat. The doctor, a two-hundred-year-old man who resembled one of the four horsemen of the Apocalypse—hadn't been sure which one at the time—told his mother that since he was there anyway, he might as well remove his tonsils.

Four days later, as his mother was packing his clothes to take him home, he had an appendicitis attack.

Talk about the bird of ill fortune dumping on you; six year old Larry had found himself immersed under a ton of shit and no, there was no pony in there anywhere.

So his fear of hospitals was not totally unwarranted. He would probably catch leprosy from a dirty needle or undergo an accidental hysterectomy. God, he wished he hadn't seen *Coma* twice.

At least his mother would have been proud of the fact he had on clean underwear when he was brought in. Terrycloth bikini shorts in red and white stripes and a blue tank top with the letters F.O. across his chest, but clean, nevertheless. Face it, pal, Mom would have had a coronary.

Last night they had stuck an IV in his arm and whisked him upstairs to a four-bed ward. He was asleep as soon as they transferred him from the gurney to the bed, but a nurse woke him almost immediately to give him two pills. He was told that they were a strong laxative; his system had to be clear for the X-ray scan first thing the next morning. The laxative was supposed to take effect in the next couple of hours, and the nurse transferred the IV bottle to a wheeled stand so he could get to the bathroom when the impulse struck.

He was wrenched out of a sound slumber at seven AM to go down to Radiology. He felt fine, no pain, but the laxative hadn't worked. The radiologist told him he had a small obstruction in his renal pelvis and showed him the X-ray. It didn't look all that small to Larry.

When he got back to the room he was hungry as hell. He pressed the button for the floor nurse and looked over at the only other occupant of the room, an old man with a back problem who had finished his breakfast and was dozing. The nurse finally showed up and Larry gave her a smile, the one with all the teeth. "You can bring my breakfast now."

"Doctor's orders, no food until after the IVP."

"Right, just had it. How about steak and eggs?" he asked hopefully.

"The doctor has to okay it first," she said mechanically.

"Well, let's get him on the horn and—"

"He's already finished rounds. He won't be back until this afternoon. If I speak with him before then, I'll try to clear it for you."

"Great," Larry grumbled as she left. "And I'll just starve to death in the interim."

By ten o'clock the nurse hadn't made an appearance, but two dozen roses were delivered by the hospital flower shop. The card read: "To Bozo the Clone, get well."

He couldn't eat the roses, but they sure made him feel a lot better.

Noon came and went. The old man was awakened for his lunch, but he fell asleep again before he could finish eating. Larry stared at the tray, trying to get up the nerve to sneak over and steal his roomy's Jello. He had swung his legs over the edge of the bed just as the dietician came in and took the tray away. Hell, he didn't like Jello that much anyway.

A few minutes later he had his first visitor. He had called the set at nine and advised Ned Vickers of his predicament. Evidently word had gotten around.

"Hello, sickie."

He looked up to see Patte Gordon leaning against the doorjamb, holding a box in one hand and a single flower in the other. "I come to help you with the funeral arrangements."

"Don't move! Just stand there in the doorway bathed in the pale glow of the phosphorescent lights. I want to remember you that way. All white and pasty."

Patte moved to the side of the bed and handed him the flower. It was metal. "That's metal."

"It's enduring," she said, grinning.

It was a carbon-steel carnation, oxidized petals surrounding BB shot pistils of brass. It was bright, beautiful, and brutal. It reminded him of Robyn.

"What's in the box?" Larry was beginning to salivate.

"Cherry cordials."

"Chocolate covered cherries!? My God, give!"

"Wait a minute, chum. You allowed to eat candy?" she said, holding the box at arm's length.

"Of course, they have me on a strict confectionary diet.

I had peanut clusters for breakfast and Mounds Bars L'Orange for lunch. Hand it over."

Larry took the box from her hands and tore it open, ripping the bright red foil from one of the cordials. He plunged it into his mouth and savored the morsel as if he might never eat again. At the rate he was going, that was a distinct possibility. "How goes it at the shop?" he asked, as he munched violently and unwrapped another candy.

"We're limping along. Vickers said if you're not back by tomorrow he's going to get you a job as H.I.C. on the *Muppet Show*."

"H.I.C.?"

"Hearing Impaired Coordinator. See, they need somebody to train the muppets to form their words more concisely."

"Ever try to lip-read a hand-held frog, right?"

"Right!" She grinned broadly and Larry was more glad to see her than he thought he would be. "You catch on fast for an invalid." She glanced over at the sleeping figure in the bed across the room. "Got yourself a real live conversationalist, huh?"

"He died three days ago but the doctor hasn't been around to certify him yet, so they keep bringing him food. Me, they're trying to starve."

Patte leaned down and smelled the roses. "Secret admirer, your wife, or the head of the network?"

"My next-door neighbor. She brought me in last night." The tone of his voice changed, and he wasn't sure if it had been at the mention of Lynn or Robyn.

"Must be serious."

"What?"

"Your neighbor lady. Can't say I've heard you mention her before."

"Yeah, well, we have a sort of mutually respectful relationship."

"Meaning you haven't slept with her yet, right?"

"Flash, sometimes you amaze me with your subtlety. If you ever start being direct, I won't recognize you."

"You going to tell me about her?"

"What's to tell?"

"When you talked about her, your face lit up like a premiere marquee. She must be some kind of lady."

Larry squirmed. "Actually, she kicked me in the side when I tried to grab her, and that's how I ended up here. The flowers were her way of apologizing."

Patte grabbed the card from the flower box before he could stop her. "Hey! That's private!"

"Bozo, huh? She's also a good judge of character, I got to give her that." Patte pulled a chair to the side of the bed and sat, taking back the box of candy. She began to unwrap a piece as she spoke. "Tell me about her and I promise to smuggle you in five pounds of fudge, disguised as a cake."

"With nuts?"

"If it's really a juicy story, you get marshmallows too."

Larry spent the next fifteen minutes bringing Patte up to date on his relationship, or lack of same, with his neighbor. She watched his face intently as he spoke, and when he finished, she asked, "So what does she really do for a living?"

"I'm not sure. For all I know, she may be a CIA. agent."

"Beware of nonpros, fella. Mixed marriages never work."

"Amen to that. Although I've heard the divorce rate in L.A. County is seventy percent these days. Maybe marriage itself doesn't work anymore."

"Have you heard the stat that most divorced men remarry within a year?"

"Not this kid. I've already had that. I don't need it again."

Patte narrowed her eyes at him. "You're a marriage

waiting to happen. Be careful of this neighbor, she may just be the one to hook you good."

Larry sat up in bed and adjusted his pillow, avoiding her penetrating gaze. "Not me, babe, I'm the proverbial bachelor. Anyway, I'm having too much fun."

"Are you?"

"What the hell is this, an inquisition? I'm lying here on my death bed and you're grilling me like a precinct sergeant from an old George Raft film. Next thing I know, you'll be bringing in Pat O'Brian to hear my confession."

"So what could it hurt?"

Larry laughed self-consciously. "I'm not so sure I should have confided in you the other night."

Patte stiffened in the chair. "I'm glad you did. You sounded pretty sorry for yourself and that may have sparked my maternal instincts. Just don't get lost in all that damn self-pity." She leaned closer and her voice softened. "You're a tender, caring, sensitive person, and you've got to keep your self-image up. You're not a loser, even if you see yourself that way sometimes. The only loser in this situation is your wife."

"Wow! That's not bad, Flash. Maybe I'd better write it down," Larry said without humor.

"Don't bother, I already did. It's the opening dialogue between Margo and Bob in the next segment, where she's trying to seduce him." She winked and smiled at him. "You didn't think I was serious, did you?"

"Have I ever?"

Patte considered that for a moment before replying. Larry wondered if she was going to take the game further, if it was a game. Maybe she just cared and it was her way of telling him so. He felt a definite magnetism in her presence, but he wasn't sure how to react to it. Dressed as she was today, in jeans and a sweater, she certainly didn't present the picture of a sex goddess. Her hair was out of place, falling over one eye, and she wore no makeup at all. But her eyes were bright, and she was here with him now. She seemed to be there often when he needed somebody to talk to, to confide in.

"No," she said with a finality that seemed sad. "Well, I best get on my horse. If you need anything, call me. You got a ride home when they pardon you?"

Larry remembered the phone number in his shirt pocket. "Yeah, that's handled, if I ever see the doctor and he gives me some kind of prognosis. If I'm still here tomorrow, I'll call you and we can go over any script problems that you and Lew can't resolve."

"Hey, you're not that indispensable."

He returned her wave as she went out into the hallway. "Sometimes I wonder."

NINE

Larry saw the doctor at two PM. He was given a prescription for a pain killer and was told that in cases like these, where the stone was small, it would probably pass normally without presenting too much of a problem. The doctor signed his release but it was too late for lunch and too early for dinner. He phoned Lynn and asked her if she could pick him up. She had been asleep, but she was in a good mood and that surprised him. Guess being sick brought out the mother in everybody.

The nurse came in with a wheelchair. He sat in it, piling his belongings in his lap. He kept the candy box, which was almost empty, and the steel flower close at hand. He placed his jacket and a spray-painted gold cane that had arrived an hour ago from the staff of *Two Families* across his lap.

He had chuckled at the card that had arrived with the gift. It read: "A little something to support you until you're *Abel*." Flash must have had a hand in that, he thought, as the nurse began to wheel him into the hallway. He waved a casual goodbye to his roommate who just went on snoring. Halfway down the corridor Larry's face took on a horrible expression of pain. "Stop!" he shouted to the nurse.

"What is it?" She leaned in over his shoulder. "Another attack?"

"Got to go to the bathroom," he said, squirming out of the chair.

He spent the next ten minutes exhausting his bowels and thanking God that the laxative hadn't hit him while he was in Lynn's car. Now that was funny. He could probably use the routine someday.

Downstairs the nurse wheeled him to the pharmacy where he had his prescription filled. As they approached the outer lobby doors, he saw Lynn strolling toward him. She was a vision of loveliness. She wore tailored black slacks and a bright red blouse opened to the second button, showing off her cleavage nicely. Her hair swirled loosely about her shoulders, and she smiled when she saw him. "Hello, you're looking a lot better than the last time I saw you."

He rose from the chair clutching his goodies and put one arm around her shoulders, supporting himself shakily with the cane. "They told me to take it easy for awhile," he lied none too convincingly. "I'm going to need a lot of care."

The nurse left with the chair, and Larry hobbled to Lynn's car taking his sweet time while he held on tight and smelled her hair. He pressed against her and watched the sunlight play off her smooth skin. When she had made him comfortable in the front seat of the BMW, he said, "Why don't we stop somewhere and I'll buy you dinner? It's the least I can do for causing you all this trouble."

"It's no trouble, and I think you'd better go home and take your medication. I can fix you something to eat."

"You don't have to do that."

"Okay."

"But if you insist, I'm too weak to argue," Larry agreed quickly.

She tilted her head and grinned. "You going to live then, I take it?"

"Not unless somebody feeds me damned soon."

She laughed. "I've got some corned beef boiling."

"All right!"

Lynn parked in the driveway and helped him inside. Then she left to see to the meal, while he showered and changed. He felt a hundred percent better, which still left him about fifty percent under par, as the needle spray of hot water played over the sore muscles in his left side. Just as he was really beginning to enjoy the shower the laxative struck again.

They sure knew what they were doing when they gave him a dose large enough to exhaust King Kong, he thought, as he sprinted for the toilet. He barely made it.

Sitting there, dripping water all over the floor, he cursed medical science in general and doctors in particular for what he thought to be a monumental lack of common sense. It had been all downhill from the day they had stopped using leeches.

When he was finished, he dressed and staggered downstairs to the phone. He called Vickers and told him he'd be in the next morning. Then he placed a call to Benny Frankel. The producer was out again, and that would have made Larry angry, but before he could lose his temper a knock sounded on the wall that separated his unit from Lynn's. That was the prearranged dinner signal. He promptly forgot all about Benny, grabbed his cane and went next door.

"Did you take your pills?" she asked, as she opened the door for him.

"Just like the doctor ordered," he replied, as he entered her town house. Her place was the flip side of his, but there the resemblance ended. The walls were done in a heavy deep blue wallpaper and white lace curtains

97

covered every window. Two large white sofas faced each other across a massive glass coffee table. Plants flourished everywhere, growing out of pots, brass tea kettles, and a large antique crib that took up one entire corner wall near the fireplace. The dining room was done in a gold brocade wallpaper, with mahogany table and chairs.

All in all, it made his place look like a vacant warehouse. "Who's your decorator?" he asked, as he admired a Chagall print above one of the sofas.

"Me. I like to experiment. Can you have anything to drink?"

"Sure. According to the doctor I'm supposed to drink five or six gallons of water a day, but you know what W.C. Fields said about that." He winked at her.

She looked at him blankly. "No, what?"

"Ah, that fish, ah, breed in it."

"Was that supposed to be funny?"

"You would have had to been there. Beer, that's it. I can drink lots of beer, if you have any."

She brought him a frosted bottle of Dos Equis and a tall delicate glass on a silver tray. "Dinner will be another half-hour. Why don't you sit down and relax?"

He took the bottle and glass and sat in a high-backed easy chair next to the fireplace. She leaned over to start the gas lighter and he admired her buttocks as they strained against the tight slacks. It was a hot day, but she had the air conditioning on and it was a comfortable sixty-five inside. The fire crackled and blazed. He leaned back and watched her as she sat cross-legged on the floor in front of the hearth and looked up at him. "Well, what part of Canada are you from?" Larry wasn't much good at small talk at the best of times, but he wanted to find out as much about her as possible.

"It still shows, huh? Alberta. I was born and raised on a ranch, got married just out of high school, and came here with my husband in the sixties." She gave him her history as if she knew he was fishing for information.

Larry looked around. "What happened to your husband?" He regretted the question the moment the words left his mouth. Subtle he wasn't, either.

"He's dead."

"I'm sorry." He was relieved, not sorry, and that made him feel miserable.

"He was killed in an auto crash ten years ago."

"Oh."

"It's all right," she assured him. "It was a long time ago."

Larry drank his beer and watched the fire. They sat quietly as if she knew he didn't feel like talking. She seemed to know how to act for every mood, a talent very few people had, but one she had developed into an art.

She rose to set the table, then brought him another beer. She was the perfect hostess throughout the meal, making enough pleasant conversation to get him talking again and catering to him like he was royalty.

The meal was a delight, tender corned beef and cabbage, boiled potatoes and carrots, with salad and a light rye bread. It was just what he needed to make him feel like a member of the human race again. He didn't even ask her for ketchup.

After she had cleared the table, refusing his help of course, they adjourned to the living room and sat on the floor in front of the fireplace, Larry with another beer, Lynn sipping Drambuie from a delicate, long-stemmed glass. "I don't watch television much," she stated honestly, "but since I met you I've made it a point to watch your show. I'd like to hear how you do it."

Larry spent the next hour explaining in minute detail how the entire TV industry revolved around his talent and creativity. Lynn listened intently, commenting occasionally and asking intelligent questions when she didn't understand a term or a piece of in-house lingoese Larry tossed about so freely. She was a real pleasure to talk to, and Larry felt comfortable with her, although her beauty still disarmed him to a great degree.

"Okay, it's your turn, Bly. What do you really do for a living?" He hadn't meant to be so blunt and it really wasn't any of his business, but the words just spilled out.

"I've got some investments, so my time is pretty much my own. My husband left me a little money and I've managed to put it to good use. I read quite a bit, walk on the beach whenever I can. I seem to be spending a good deal of time in antique shops lately."

Christ, she was financially independant too. What more could a man ask? "You're not in real estate, are you?"

"Not to a great extent, although I do own a few pieces of property. Why?"

"Oh, my, ah, wife, she's in that trade . . ." he sputtered. He was sorry he had brought up the subject.

"You want to tell me about her?" Lynn asked casually.

"Not particularly. She and I don't get along well since our separation. Hell, we don't get along at all."

"Any children?"

"Two boys." Larry struggled to change the direction of the conversation. "How about you?"

"No, I'm not able to have any more children."

"Any more?" Larry looked around again. He hadn't seen any evidence of kids, pictures or the like.

"I had twin girls. They would have been twelve this year."

"Would have been?"

"They were in the car with my husband." It was an informative statement that held no emotion.

"I *am* sorry."

"Thanks, but it's okay. As I said, time tends to wash away old memories. I think you'll find that out for yourself.

100

Right now you may hate your wife, but give yourself some time and that opinion may change."

"Fat chance."

It was beginning to get dark, but Lynn made no effort to turn on the lights. She shook her head and the firelight danced behind the waves and curls, giving her a halolike aura. "You hated her all those years you were married to her?"

"Of course not!" Larry was starting to get irritated. "Just since I found out what she really was."

"There must have been some good times," Lynn said softly.

"I can't seem to recall any right off hand." It was difficult for him to be bitter when talking to Lynn. He tried, but it was almost impossible.

"People do grow apart, you know. They form different interests, different social structures. She's not the same woman she was fifteen years ago—or fifteen months ago." Larry noticed a certain self-reflection to her tone, so he didn't reply. He'd probably learn more about her just by listening. "You might try to understand her motives, if you wanted to."

"You don't even know what she did to me."

"I don't have to. I just don't think people are entirely bad, or good for that matter. We all do things we don't like, things we regret. Maybe your wife did what she did because she had no other choice. Maybe if you gave her a chance she'd at least become your friend."

"That'll be the day. You offer that woman a little compassion and she'd either sell it, list it, or appraise it."

Lynn ignored his flip answer. "Well, it's none of my business, but it seems to me that if you remain resentful for the rest of your life, you're the one that suffers for it." She rose abruptly. "Can I get you another beer?"

"No, I really should go take my pills and lie down for

awhile." He put his glass down on the coffee table and hoisted his weary body out of the chair. He didn't want to leave her, but he was feeling shitty and he didn't want to be sick in front of her.

She walked him to the door as he said, "Would you like to go out for dinner sometime, so I can repay you for all your help?"

"You don't owe me anything, DiaMonte. I did it because you were in trouble and I like you."

That threw him. It was an honest statement and he wasn't prepared for it. "It's an old Sicilian custom. Humor me?"

"Why should I?"

"Because I like you too." He realized as he spoke that he really did like her. The attraction certainly wasn't sexual; the way he felt right now he didn't think he could get it up if she started to strip right there in the entry hall.

She opened the door for him. "Let me think about it."

"That's fair. And thanks again."

He stepped onto the walkway and was ten feet away when she called out to him. "Larry?"

He stopped and turned, knowing instinctively that she had changed her mind and wanted to set a definite date. "Yeah?"

"You forgot your cane." She walked over and handed it to him.

"Right, thanks."

Larry DiaMonte leaned heavily on the gold cane as he made his way home.

TEN

"You evasive son of a bitch! Why the hell haven't you returned my calls for the last week?" Larry shouted into the phone. He was alone in his office the next Monday morning, and between the trips to the bathroom every three minutes and the pain in his side, he was not a man to be trifled with.

"I've been busy," Benny Frankel said unapologetically. "Sorry to hear about your kidney stone thing. Seems to be an occupational hazard these days. Too much sex, I think."

"Just messenger over my script and do me one favor, Benny?"

"What?"

"Get fucked."

"Ah, yes, the script. What was it called? *Thirty Seconds Over Hollywood*?"

"It's been so long I can't remember. Just send it back and I'll peddle it to somebody with a little class."

"How would you like to take a meeting with Kent Jacobs?" Benny's tone was smug, and Larry had to admit that was one hell of a good conversation stopper. Jacobs was one of the top ten, a box office draw that would just about assure the earning ability of any film he was involved with. His last two pictures, fairly medium-budget action comedies, had people queing up for blocks around every exhib in the country.

"You wouldn't put on a lifelong friend, somebody that went to P.S. 15 with you?" Larry's attitude had undergone a marked change.

Frankel laughed. "I never went to grammar school. I'm a self-made man. And yes, I would send you up if I thought it would do any good. Kent's in Bimini relaxing. I got the script to him, he read it, and called me this morning."

"What did he say?"

"Not a hell of a lot. Just that he wondered if you'd take a meeting with him."

"Whatever happened to 'have a meeting' or 'meet with'?"

"The jargon is constantly changing, old boy. You got to stay in the mainstream. You've been in TV too long, Lar. Keeping up with the in-group lingo is essential in the film biz. Shall I tell Kent you're too busy with your Saturday morning cartoon show?"

Larry was stalling, trying to compose himself so he wouldn't seem too anxious. "I can't just pick up and fly off to Bimini this afternoon, Benny. They'd charge me import duty on my kidney stone."

Benny laughed. "Not to worry, he'll be in town over the weekend to see Bethany. She's due in from Canada in a few days."

Bethany Drew Jacobs was Kent's outspoken wife who had made a couple of mildly successful pictures a few years ago. Her performances had been well received and it looked like she was on her way to stardom when she met and married Kent. Now she did some summer stock and an occasional guest shot on TV, but she was mostly involved in saving the humpback whale or other vague causes that Larry couldn't understand and didn't bother keeping track of. "Tell him I'd be honored," Larry said finally.

"Good. It'll probably be Sunday, 'cause she's flying in Saturday and he wants her to sit in."

"What the fuck for?"

"I don't know. I didn't ask him."

"What the hell do you do?"

"Make very successful films. Whatta you do?"

"Right, I get the message. Let me know where and when."

"His place in Trancas. I'll get back to you about the time."

Larry hung up and leaned back in his chair. Now why in God's name did Jacobs want to meet with him? Was he going to make an offer on *Five'll Get You Ten?* More than likely Kent had read the script and was going to give him some sound advice: become a plumber.

Larry was taking two Coedine #3 tablets every couple of hours. The prescription called for one every two hours, but he was feeling miserable. He went to see his regular urologist, Dr. Rehme, that afternoon, because of the appearance of blood in his urine. That had scared the piss out of him, literally.

The good doctor had nodded a lot and told him the massive pressure he felt when he urinated was due to the stone moving to his bladder. If everything went normally, the stone should pass soon. "You want me to operate?" Rehme asked him.

"Hell no!"

"That's nice, because I'm not much good at that sort of thing. Too many people nowadays feel that going under the knife is the only solution to all their ills," he stated in his cracker barrel manner. "I'm glad to see you're among the intelligent minority."

Larry wasn't all that sure he should have discounted the idea of surgery. The only thing that allowed him to grin and bear it was the horror stories he had heard. The ghastly tales of the grappling hook devices they stuck up your penis to fish for obstructions. That he could do without, at least for the time being.

On the way out he stopped at Rehme's med-assistant's desk to say goodbye to Jan. The attractive young lady in the starched white uniform and blue sweater looked up and grinned. "I hope you're feeling better soon, Mr. DiaMonte. One of these days I'm going to see what your smile looks like."

"This *is* my smile." Larry grimaced, then snapped his fingers and frowned. "Damn, I forgot to ask Jeff something."

He started back up the long hallway lined with doors, but Jan called after him, "He's already with another patient. Maybe I can answer your question."

Larry came back to her desk. "Ah, it's kinda delicate."

Jan laughed. "Oh, that. Does it hurt when you do it?

He hesitated. "Well, no, not exactly."

"Then if I were you, I'd do it till it hurts."

Sound advice, thought Larry. And free too. "What I really need is a live-in nurse. Care to apply for the position?"

Jan made a face at him. "Just don't forget to use the strainer and bring the stone in when you pass it. We have to send it to the lab to be analyzed."

"You sure you won't reconsider?"

"That depends on how big it is," she said slyly.

"How big what is?" Larry feigned ignorance. The two of them had flirted on each of his visits, and now it was a kind of ritual.

"The kidney stone, dummy. If it's a real monster, then

106

you might need a nurse to help you recover."

He waved as he went to the door. "I do feel like I own a piece of the rock. See you soon."

Larry phoned Lynn and invited her to watch *Two Families* at his place later that evening. She had been hesitant at first, telling him that she was expecting a call and might have to go out. He was persistant and she finally gave in, agreeing to come over by nine.

He went home early and bustled around, straightening up the place and watering the plants. The fern on the hall stand was beyond help, he decided, after staring at it for several moments. He threw it in the garbage and made a mental note to pick up something with a little greater longevity. Something that would last a month instead of the usual five days.

He was groggy from the medication he'd been taking all day and it didn't seem to be helping much. The pain was worse than it had been, and he was worried. He didn't feel much like eating, so he took a nap on the couch. The doorbell woke him out of the soundest sleep he had had in ten days. He looked at the digital clock atop the TV set. Eight forty-five. Must be Lynn.

"Welcome to the infirmary," he said, as he opened the door trying to look the picture of good health. She stood there with a big smile on her face. He felt better already.

"Am I on time?" she beamed.

"Sure. Get you a drink?" He closed the door as she walked to the living room.

"What are you having?"

Larry shrugged as he followed her. "I shouldn't mix alcohol with the pills. But don't let my delicate condition spoil your evening."

"Maybe a soft drink, if you have one."

Dammit, she did it again, making him feel that if he couldn't drink, then neither would she. The perfect woman. He went into the kitchen and opened the refrigerator door. "How are you doing?" she called from the living room.

"I feel like I died yesterday." He fumbled around and came up with a single Diet Pepsi. "Don't let that bother you. I'm beginning to accept it as a standard condition."

He poured the soft drink into a tall glass and added ice. Then he joined her on the sofa. Picking up the remote control he turned the set on, but kept the sound low. They made small talk about his illness and the upcoming episode of *Two Families* until nine, when Larry reached over and turned up the sound. He had already seen the show several times on tape so he studied her face as she watched the opening scenes. She was a good audience. The show was "sweetened," but that didn't seem to bother her as much as it did him. She chuckled at all the right times, but she didn't respond to the laugh track like a programmed monkey. He liked that.

During the first commercial spot she turned to him and said, "What's a Claymore mine?"

That's when he kissed her. He took her completely by surprise when he leaned over. She didn't have time to pull away. Her lips were soft and pliant, and he applied pressure as he waited for her to part them. She didn't. Not to be deterred he put his arm around her shoulder and pulled her closer. What the hell? If he were going to die tomorrow, what did it matter?

Her hand came up and touched his cheek lightly, barely brushing his beard, and he thought she was going to return the passion he was feeling, but she pulled back suddenly, breaking contact.

"It's a metal-contained explosive," he said, answering her question as if nothing had happened, "that you put on

108

the ground in hopes that your enemies will step on it and blow themselves to hell."

"Thank you."

They watched the rest of the show in silence while he wondered what she had been thanking him for. He left the TV on until the credit crawl spread his name all over the large screen. Might as well try to impress her if he could. Flicking the off switch he turned to her. "Well, what did you think?"

"I thought it was very good." Again he looked for a double meaning in her words. "The lady realtor sure was a bitch, though."

That was the first time he had heard her swear. Maybe she was beginning to feel more comfortable with him. "Yeah," he sighed. "She sure was."

The phone rang at exactly nine thirty-two. He smiled as he pulled himself painfully to his feet. Didn't have to be no psychic to figure out who that was. "Excuse me, this won't take long."

He walked to his desk and lifted the receiver. "Good evening, Larry DiaMonte, boy writer at your service," he said sweetly.

"You bastard!" Robyn's voice was like cold flint.

"Why, hello there."

"You've done some rotten things to me before, Larry, but this is the lowest."

The innocence in his tone would have made Don Rickles look like Don Ho. "I haven't got the faintest idea what you're referring to." He glanced over and smiled at Lynn. She smiled back.

"You mother-fucking cocksucker!"

"Oh oh, easy, babe. You can't sway me with words of endearment anymore. Save 'em for your lover. That's probably the only way he can get it up."

Suddenly Larry had the overwhelming urge to go to the

109

bathroom. Instead he sat in the desk chair and crossed his legs tightly. That would have to wait, he wouldn't miss this conversation for an Emmy nomination.

"I'll get you for this one, Larry. I promise you that."

He inhaled through his teeth and said seriously, "And just how do you plan to do that?"

He could hear her seething on the other end of the line. He knew she was trying to calm herself. Finally she said, "Your two sons watched that program. How do you feel about that?"

Ouch! Home run. She hadn't forgotten how to play dirty. "I think it's about time they found out what kind of person you really are. Let me ask you something, Rob. What do they think when your lover crawls onto my bed and spends the night? Does the moaning and whispering keep them awake all night, or do you tie and gag them so they won't bother you?"

"I'm not going to let you get away with this one," she screamed, ignoring his question.

"Oh, you're not, huh? Well, in case you're interested, the network liked tonight's show so much they've given me the okay to write a pilot for the new character."

"What are you going to call it, *Hate Is Enough?*

Larry couldn't help himself. He burst into a fit of laughter and grabbed at his crotch. "Hey, that's not bad, Rob. Evidently you haven't lost your sense of humor completely."

Her tone changed. "Why do you treat me like I'm inhuman? I'm not, you know. I'm the mother of your children and anything you do to hurt me hurts them too."

Larry sighed deeply. She often used that tack when all else failed. The "pity me and the kids" routine that used to make him feel about three inches tall. But this time he knew her for the coldblooded opportunist she really was. "Rob, I just have one thing to say to you."

"What?"

"I got to take a piss." Larry hung up before she could reply and leapt for the downstairs bathroom, slamming the door behind him. The pressure in his penis was enormous, and it seemed to increase rather than lessen as the stream of urine splashed into the toilet bowl. Then it was like a dam breaking; the pressure ceased suddenly and he heard something *clink* against the porcelain of the bowl.

He zipped his pants and let out a sigh of relief. Going to his hands and knees, he waited for the yellowish water to clear. Sure enough, there was something there, distorted by the refraction of the water. A grayish, elongated lump nestled at the bottom of the bowl. He rolled up his sleeve, said, "Yuck," and fished around the bowl until he came up with the stone.

He struck his hand under the sink faucet up to the wrist and rinsed it, then held the stone up to the light to scrutinize the cause of all his pain. Jesus! It was the size of a .22 slug.

There was a knock on the bathroom door. "Are you all right?"

His penis was a little sore, but all in all, he felt like a new man. And he had forgotten all about Lynn. He flushed the toilet and opened the door, extending the stone under her nose. "That, my dear, is the little bastard that's been causing all the trouble."

"It's gigantic!" she exclaimed as she leaned in to get a closer look.

"Goes with the territory," Larry laughed.

"How do you feel?"

Larry did a little soft-shoe step. "I feel good, good, good! Fantastic! I think I'll have it bronzed and send it to the NASA museum. A small stone for DiaMonte, a giant boulder for mankind!"

111

Larry went into the kitchen and dropped the stone into a baggie, then placed it in the center of his desk top. He made a drink and settled back on the couch with Lynn. "Let's celebrate."

"What would you like to do?" Lynn asked sincerely.

He repressed the reply he wanted to make and said, "You really want to know?"

Lynn shook her head. "I may be sorry I asked."

"I'd like to go out for a pepperoni and olive pizza, then go for a walk on the beach."

Lynn's face lighted up like a full moon coming out from behind a cloudbank. "That's funny, I was just thinking the same thing."

ELEVEN

They stopped at a Shakies in Santa Monica, then drove on to Venice, the aroma of warm pizza filling the interior of the Porsche. Larry parked the car near the boardwalk and he trudged out on the sand followed by Lynn, the pizza box in one hand, and a six-pack of Heineken in the other.

Larry stopped near the long rock pier and removed the car blanket from his shoulder. Spreading the plaid blanket under the cupola of starlight he opened the pizza box and two bottles of the cold beer. "Madam—" he gestured in his best impression of the Dome maitre d'— "dinner is served."

They attacked the large pizza like hungry wolves, swigging the beer between bites, and discussing the beauty of the ocean around mouthfuls of pepperoni.

Lynn wiped her lips on a white paper napkin and dropped the last crust into the long flat box. "Thank you, sir. That was a meal fit for a king."

"Yeah, the king of Uganda."

"Hey, writer, every once in a while you have to get your feet in the sand and your hands greasy. Don't knock it."

Larry rose and reached down for her hands. "Come on, let's go for a walk."

The night was cool but the sand still retained much of the day's heat. They kicked off their shoes and strolled along the water's edge, the incoming tide threatening their bare feet. "You do much fishing?" Lynn asked abstractly.

"Not me. Never had the patience for it."

"My Uncle Fred used to take me fishing all the time in our front yard."

"You had water in your front yard?"

"No, but he'd fill a bucket and then cover the bottom with nuts and bolts. I was four, and he'd talk to me for hours about the ocean. Then he'd distract me by pointing at a bird or something, and when my attention was away from the bucket he'd lean over and hook a bolt with my line and yell, 'Lindy, you got something!'" Her face took on a faraway look. "Then we'd both laugh as I reeled in a rusty old piece of metal. He'd dry it off carefully and put it aside, and then we'd start again."

"Ever get your limit?" Larry asked.

"No, he used to say it didn't matter what you caught as long as you were serious about fishing." She stopped and looked over at Larry. "I really loved that old man. He was a crazy dreamer." She paused and took his hand. "You remind me a lot of him."

A giant wave washed around them unexpectedly and Larry yelped loudly and jumped back. Lynn stood laughing at him as the white foam swirled around her ankles and up her calves, soaking her dress. Even with her hair out of place and her shoes gripped tightly in one hand and her hem pasted against her knees, she looked regal. As if Princess Grace had decided to take the day off and go out to play.

"Chicken!" she shouted at him as he skipped back to avoid another wave. Larry was watching the next crest swell behind her. It was a monster.

114

"Oh yeah!" he yelled, as he advanced toward her. Scooping up a handful of water he menaced her with his cupped hands. She backed as he knew she would and was slammed by the surging wave. She screamed as the cold water struck her hips, soaking her whole body and making her dress stick to her like flypaper.

They stared at each other as the water receded, then she sat down in the mud and began laughing uncontrollably. Larry grabbed her by the shoulders and lifted her to her feet, holding her shivering frame against his side as he led her up the beach. Throwing the blanket around her, he packed up the remnants of their meal. "Come on, you'll catch pneumonia unless I get you in front of a blazing fire and pour some brandy into you."

She didn't resist, and forty-five minutes later they were sitting in front of Larry's fireplace with glasses in their hands. Lynn's clothing was draped all over the downstairs bathroom and she wore Larry's terrycloth robe. She could have stopped at her place and changed, but somehow the subject never came up.

She placed her brandy glass on the hearth and drew her knees up to her chin, hugging them with her arms as she looked at him. "I couldn't help overhearing your end of the phone conversation. You really love her, don't you?"

"Who?" Larry was taken by surprise. The last thing in the world he was thinking about was Robyn.

"Your wife."

He gulped his drink and stared into the fire. "Hell no."

Lynn shrugged. "All right, I won't bring it up again if you don't want to talk about it." Then she tilted her head to one side and her serious expression dissolved into a grin that was warmer than the fire. "You're a nice guy, Larry DiaMonte. It's too bad we didn't meet sooner."

"Why, you getting married in the morning or something?"

"Would I tell you if I were?" she said merrily.

Larry looked into her deep brown eyes. Next to Robyn's brackish personality, this woman was a bright, vivacious, thrilling lady. Yeah, she was right. It was too bad they hadn't met sooner. "I want to apologize for kissing you like that earlier. I don't know what possessed me." He had absolutely no idea why he had just made that statement. He wasn't sorry. As a matter of fact, he was thinking seriously about doing it again.

"Did you kiss me?" she teased. "I hadn't noticed."

"I'm that memorable, huh?"

"A Claymore mine," she said mechanically, "is a metal-contained explosive that you put on the ground in hopes that your enemies will step on it and blow themselves to h—"

She didn't have the chance to finish, because Larry slid closer and kissed her. This time she opened her mouth and sucked in his tongue as she threw her arms around his neck. Larry eased her back slowly on one of the big pillows and straightened out her legs with one hand, bringing her body up firm against his.

Her breathing was labored and her eyes were glazed through half-closed lids. Larry came up for air, but didn't break contact. He ran his tongue over her full lower lip, then around her nose, finally kissing both her eyelids. She sighed and brought her hands down to his chest, pushing against him weakly. "I've got to go."

"Right." Before she could protest again he covered her mouth with his and ran his hands over her back, kneading the taut muscles in her shoulders. She moaned and relaxed a little, but she was still tense.

"I really should—" she began as he opened the robe and ran the palm of his hand lightly over one nipple. She closed her eyes and put her head back, moaning helplessly. "I . . . my God . . . that feels good . . ."

116

He increased the pressure and moved his hand in a large circle over both breasts, then lowered his head and took a nipple between his lips. He played with it, nudging it back and forth with his tongue, then took a third of her breast in his mouth and sucked hard. "Yes . . . yes . . ." she almost shouted. "Please don't stop . . ."

He continued licking her breast while he tried to unbutton his shirt with one hand, tearing it in the process. Placing his bare chest hard against her breasts he tucked up his knees and fumbled his belt buckle open. With one hand behind his back he pulled mightily and his Levi's slipped down over his buttocks. He kicked them away. He wasn't wearing shorts and his erect penis jabbed against her leg. He looked down at the soft tangle of hair between her thighs and kissed her nipples again as he ran his hand over her moisture.

She had stopped talking now and her breathing was rapid, like a woman who wanted it badly, but hadn't had it in a long time. She seemed frightened and he stroked her hair to allay that fear. When she had calmed down he entered her. It was as if her whole body erupted when he pushed into her. She arched her back and lifted her pelvis high to meet him, a low wailing sound issuing from deep inside her throat.

Larry gasped as her fingernails dug into his back and scratched him through the material of his shirt. He put the pain out of his mind as he thrust into her, slowly at first, because he wanted it to be good for her too. But his control quickly disappeared as her rhythmic convulsions forced him deeper into her body. Her animal fury almost flung him from her on the outward strokes, then she went suddenly rigid and bit his ear. He felt her vagina pulse around his throbbing penis, and he came with her in the most excruciating climax he had ever experienced.

He rolled to his side, but kept his penis inside her,

kissing the tip of her nose. "You certainly get carried away," he panted, not knowing what else to say. "I thought for a minute there you were going to bite my ear off."

She kissed his ear. "If I hurt you, why didn't you speak up?"

"I didn't want to break your mood by screaming."

"Thank you."

She laughed and hugged him close, nuzzling his neck with her nose. "I never thought I'd experience anything like that again," she commented, as she ran a hand over his cheek. "You're one hell of a man, DiaMonte."

"And you, Ms. Singer, are one stand-up lady."

"Hmmmm, that's the way I should have stayed, standing up." Then the satisfied expression on her face turned to a dark frown. "I shouldn't have let this happen." She pulled away, and his limp penis slid out of her and flopped against his thigh. "I've got to go."

"Now wait a damn minute. The night's still young. We just started—"

She jumped up and ran for the door, pulling the robe tight around her. Larry wasn't sure in the dim light, but it looked as if she were crying. "What about your clothes?" But she was out the door, leaving him lying there on the rug in just his shirt and socks. He felt ridiculous.

Now what the hell was that all about? She couldn't have been celibate for the last ten years. That was abnormal. But then, what's normal?

Larry shook his head. She hates herself, pal, because she let you make love to her so soon. She's really not that kind of girl, you stupid asshole! You could have waited. You may have really screwed things up with her for good.

All of a sudden he was exhausted. Too many things had happened today. He rose, lit a cigarette, and picked up his pants. His crotch was still damp and he wiped at it with his Levi's as he headed for the stairs.

118

As he passed the answering machine he stopped. There was one message registered in the little round window. He hit the rewind button, then keyed playback. A thickly German-accented voice that he recognized immediately as Patte's came from the speaker. "Dis ess Eva Braun. Addy and I vill be at zee bunker number oontil quite late." Larry chuckled as the tape ran on. "Seriously, sports fans, if you get in before midnight, give me a call. If you need somebody to talk to."

The tape ended and Larry shut off the machine. He looked at the clock on the TV. It was twelve fifteen. So much for timing.

As he started up the stairs to bed he glanced at the roses Lynn had sent him at the hospital. They were in a vase on the kitchen counter. They were dead.

Beside the vase, the carbon-steel carnation he had stuck in an old coffee cup looked as healthy as ever.

TWELVE

Larry slept like a man two weeks dead. When he awoke, he felt completely refreshed, hungry as hell, and ready to take on the world. He rolled over and picked up the phone from the night stand beside the bed and punched Lynn's number. It was nine fifteen and he was late for work, but he let the phone ring for a full minute before he replaced the receiver.

He got out of bed and showered and dressed. Going downstairs he toasted two English muffins, spread them with margarine and grape jelly, and poured a glass of orange juice. When he had finished his breakfast he called Lynn again. No answer. He banged on the wall a couple of times then rolled a sheet of twenty-pound bond into his IBM Selectric and began to slowly punch the keys:

DEAR MS. SINGER,

I would like to formally apologize for my conduct of last evening. I would not blame you if you never wanted to see me again. There are some things that can be forgiven and then there are other actions that are so reprehensible that they can only be justified by a plea of mental derangement.

* * *

What I did last night falls into the latter category, but if you do decide to forgive me on the grounds of temporary insanity, I promise, on my sainted mother's head, that it will never, never, never happen again.

I will never do it again, under pain of death, expulsion from WGA West, or worse; mix pepperoni and olives.

BOZO THE CLONE

He scribbled his initials on the bottom of the paper and folded it into an envelope. On the way out he leaned on her doorbell several times. Then he stuck the envelope between the branches of a potted plant beside her door where she couldn't miss it.

He drove to the office and spent the day working on the final draft of the Christmas two-parter. Patte didn't bring up her phone call of the previous evening, so he refrained from mentioning it.

The afternoon dragged on with him looking at his watch every ten minutes. He called Lynn several times, but got no answer. Finding it difficult to concentrate, he gave his notes to Lew and Patte to apply the final touches, then went home early.

As he pulled into his street he saw Lynn backing the BMW out of her garage. He downshifted into first and braked with a squeal of tires as he swung the Porsche sideways in the street, blocking her egress. Just like in the movies, he grinned. Now he'd get her attention. Getting out, he leaned on the side of the car facing the on-coming BMW. He crossed his arms and smiled as the car accelerated toward him.

121

But, just like in real life, the street was wide and the Porsche was short. She gunned her car around his without so much as a sideward glance, leaving him standing there looking like a fool.

Saturday morning.

Larry had been standing in front of the upstairs bedroom window for over an hour. The window overlooked the driveways, and he peered through the Venetian blinds, waiting patiently. He had concocted a simple, yet devious plan that he was sure would work. He had tried all week to get in touch with Lynn, but she had avoided him like he was a process server. He was desperate.

He had parked the Porsche two feet over his driveway line so that his front bumper blocked Lynn's garage door. When she keyed the opener from inside the door would rise about a foot, then stop when it came into contact with the underside of his front bumper. She would then have to call him to move his car if she wanted to go out. It was the perfect plot. Nothing could go wrong.

He smiled as he slid the glass balcony door open. Stepping out on the balcony he leaned on the low wrought-iron railing so he would be in a better position to observe the action. He didn't have long to wait.

He heard the electric motor hum to life and watched the door begin what he knew would be an abortive ascent. But, instead of hitting the bottom of the bumper, the corner of the heavy door smashed his right turn signal to bits and took out the parking light, leaving a long scar on the fender.

"Ohhhhh shit!" he shouted as he took the stairs three at a time and ran out the front door. Coming to a stop up against the Porsche he reached in and eased up on the parking brake, let the car roll back a few feet, then secured the brake again. He was standing there surveying the damage and cursing under his breath as the door rose. Lynn stared at him from inside the garage, a look of total surprise on her face.

"See what you did to my car?" he yelled. "You crushed it! Don't you look where you're going when you open the door, f'chrissake?"

"How was I supposed to know your car was parked in front of my door?" she shouted back.

"Because you should have known I'd stoop to anything to talk to you. I considered sleeping on your doorstep last night, but it was too damn cold." Looking at her trim figure was beginning to have a calming effect on him. He spoke a little more normally as he continued. "I even thought about cutting a hole in our common wall and sneaking in on you in the middle of the night."

"Why didn't you?" She finally smiled.

"Because I used that bit on my show a month ago, and I like to keep my material fresh." He winked at her. "Besides, my butter knife kept bending."

She laughed and he knew he had her. "What do I have to do to preserve the integrity of my home? Pick up some Claymore mines?"

"That's one option."

"I get a choice, huh?"

"Yep. Go out to dinner with me tonight," he said quickly. "Just dinner and a film or whatever. I promise you, no hands, no pizza, and no commitments."

She shook her head and this time the lightness was gone from her tone. "I can't. I've got a date."

"Break it."

She hesitated as if she were making the most difficult decision of her life. Don't let her rationalize it, dummy, or you'll end up alone again, or worse yet, with Branda. "If you don't go out with me tonight, I'll have another kidney stone. Then you'll be sorry."

"You know, if you had passed that thing a few hours later, you could have killed me with it," she said brightly.

Larry wanted to laugh hysterically, but he figured he better not take the chance. "Then it's a date?"

"If I say yes, do we get to do what I want to do?"

Here it comes, champ. She wants to spend the night in bed and the hell with dinner, Larry assured himself. "Just name it. An eight-course gourmet meal? A charter flight to Acapulco? What?"

"I'd like to play miniature golf."

"You're kidding?"

"Nope. It's something I haven't done for years. Are you sorry you asked me?"

"Lady, if you said you wanted to go horseback riding right now, I'd put a saddle on my back. You're faded."

"All right, if you'll move your car, I'll be ready at seven."

"Good. I'll pick you up at five." He spread his hands, palms out, and shrugged. "Might as well get an early start."

By five thirty they were teeing off on the first hole at Golfland. It was beginning to get dark and the course lights were just coming on. Larry approached a dragon head with a gaping mouth that was a par four and frowned as he lined up for the shot. He was wearing an old pair of white jeans with varnish stains on the knees and a battered turtleneck sweater. He hit the ball and it flew off the green and ended up in a pond fifty feet away.

Lynn doubled up with laughter and moved in to swing. She was dressed in a soft cashmere sweater and slacks and looked like a high-fashion model on a coffee break. Larry noted the stares of the other golfers, both men and women, and he felt terrific.

She was having a good time, so Larry hadn't made any mention of their night together. He just joked and kept

124

score, trying to concentrate on the course rather than her body. When they reached the last hole her body was ahead by fifteen strokes.

He totaled the score, initialed the bottom of the card and handed it to her with a ceremonious bow. She accepted her win gracefully, and he carried the clubs as they walked back to the arcade. She grabbed his arm as they passed the nineteenth hole, a straight ramp where the players attempted to win a free game by slamming the ball into an elevated circle about the size of a demitasse cup. "Aren't you going to try it?" she asked, as she tugged him toward the tree.

"Hell no. I could never win anything." He tilted his head and gauged the incline of the ramp. "Impossible shot. We're wasting our time."

She took a club from him, placed the ball in the worn spot on the astroturf, and swung. The orange spheroid missed the circle by two feet and disappeared into one of the side troughs. "See what I mean?" Larry said, as he put his green ball down and wound up to swing. "Arnold Palmer couldn't hit that thing."

He struck the ball and without looking to see where it went, turned back to Lynn. Before he could open his mouth to say, See, I told you so, the bell went off and the clamor echoed all over the course. "I'll be damned!" he said, as Lynn shrieked and grabbed him around the neck, kissing him soundly.

Larry threw back his shoulders and smiled. "You see, the method is in precomputing the trajectory." He gestured as he walked her back to the club shack. "A trained eye can line up the shot in a millisecond, then all it takes is superior coordination and perfect wrist control."

"Blind luck, huh?" she chuckled.

"Exactly. But trained, practiced blind luck."

They drove home to change for dinner. As he opened

the passenger door of the car, he said, "Let's have a drink before we go."

She didn't protest too strongly, and once inside he went to the bar and took a pitcher of dry martinis from the bar refrigerator. He poured the chilled liquor into a glass and handed it to her. Just as he was about to fix one for himself, the phone rang.

It was Benny Frankel. "Larry, I'm out at Kent's place. He wants to meet now."

"Now? Jesus, I thought it was set for tomorrow."

"Now. I told him you could be here in forty-five minutes."

"I'm busy tonight, Ben," he said, as he looked over at Lynn sitting on the couch sipping her drink. "Can't you postpone it till tomorrow?"

"You want to write movies or what?"

Larry considered the statement for a moment. "I'm bringing a friend, okay?"

"I don't care if you bring your goldfish, just get your ass out here fast." Benny gave him the directions to Jacob's house in Trancas, and Larry hung up.

He walked to the sofa, removed the glass from Lynn's hand, and set it on the coffee table. Taking her by the shoulders he hoisted her to her feet. "Come on, lady. We're going for a ride."

"Where?"

"If I told you, you'd probably want two days to dress. Let's go."

Once they were in the car and moving Larry explained where they were headed and why. He figured she wouldn't chance jumping at seventy miles an hour.

"But I thought you were a TV writer," Lynn said, after she calmed down enough to realize she was stuck with the situation.

Larry stared straight ahead and fished a cigarette out of

126

the pack on the dash. "Contrary to public opinion, Singer, the two are not mutually exclusive."

"Well, I'm sure if you wrote it, it's funny."

Larry frowned and pushed in the dash lighter. "It's a serious drama with comedic overtones. Something I've always wanted to do. I found it a hell of a lot harder than hitting a punch line every thirty seconds, but I enjoyed it more. It left me with a real feeling of accomplishment, like I finally did something worthwhile." He glanced over at her profile in the light from the instrument panel. "Can you understand that?"

"Maybe better than you think," she said softly.

"Well, it ain't *Going in Style,* but I think it could be a good, entertaining film. Aw, what the hell do I know? I thought till recently being bisexual meant you had intercourse twice a year," he added, as he smiled over at her.

She groaned properly and took his hand and squeezed it. "The lousy joke notwithstanding, I think I know how you feel."

Kent Jacobs's house nestled in a clump of woods. Larry steered the Porsche up the long driveway and brought it to a halt in front of the sprawling three-story mansion. The arenalike parking area looked like a Mercedes dealership. He edged his car in next to one of the 450 SLC's and he and Lynn walked up the long path to the front door.

A young Mexican girl opened the door for them and let them into an entry hall that was as big as Larry's whole house. He gawked at the paintings and pieces of sculpture that graced the long hall as he and Lynn followed the servant into a librarylike study. The Library of Congress, Larry decided, as he looked at the floor-to-ceiling bookshelves and the old monastery reading tables.

A group of people dressed in evening wear were standing around several sofas at the end of the room near a large fireplace. Larry looked down at his stained pants and sighed. He felt like a Nazi soldier at a VFW meeting, and for a second he considered turning on his heel and leaving. Until Bethany Drew smiled at him. She was sitting on a circular rust-colored sofa with her husband beside her, perched on the arm of the couch with a glass in his hand. She wore a black silk dress, and a black turban covered her usually fluffy hair.

Kent Jacobs stood and straightened the lapel of his velour dinner jacket and got up to greet the new arrivals. "Welcome. Sorry I couldn't give you more notice," he said with a slight drawl. He was several inches over six feet in height, and his jet-black hair and mustache seemed to shine in the glare from the massive chandelier that dangled like a hovering helicopter overhead. He extended his hand to Lynn and smiled, then kissed her hand as she placed it in his.

"That's all right," mumbled Larry. "Ah, I'd like you to meet Lynn Singer.

Jacobs still held Lynn's hand. "My pleasure."

Benny Frankel was leaning against the fireplace with Jennifer. Benny had been right, she was all tits and ass, but the way they were arranged under the white lace-layered evening dress was a real show stopper. Benny came across the large room and guided the trio back to the sofas. "Glad you could make it," he said, then introduced Lynn and Larry to Ray Cline, a slender man in his thirties with wild hair and an intense bearing who was Kent's business manager. Cline and Frankel both wore tuxedos, and Larry was beginning to get nervous.

A look of recognition passed between Cline and Lynn, but both remained formal. Larry couldn't help notice it, but he was too jittery to let it register consciously.

The sixth member of the group, a youngish beauty who was obviously Cline's companion, nodded at the intro-

128

ductions. Her name was Mary or Gerry, or something that Larry didn't quite catch. It looked like a party was just about to begin, or just winding up. Lynn sat down beside Bethany and they began an animated conversation almost immediately. Larry watched them as Kent made small talk about how good it was to be home. Then he turned to a bartender that Larry hadn't noticed before. The man stood behind the long bar that took up one entire wall to the rear of the sofas. Kent ordered champagne all around as Larry brought his gaze back to the two women. Next to Bethany, Lynn looked right at home. As a matter of fact, Larry admitted, Lynn looked more like a movie star in her casual clothing than Drew did dressed to the nines.

The bartender handed glasses to Larry and Lynn. Jacobs raised his in a toast. "To a good script, the basis of a first-rate film."

"I'll drink to that," Larry said, as he gulped his champagne.

Jacobs sipped at his drink and said, "So much for the cordiality. Beth, why don't you show the ladies around?"

Bethany rose and took Lynn's hand. "Come on, it's the only chance I get to impress people." They walked out of the library like college roommates with the other two women trailing close behind. When the four men were alone Jacobs ordered brandy, then dismissed the bartender. Taking a seat in the center of the large sofa with Frankel on his right and Cline to his left he faced Larry, who settled into a high-backed chair, feeling like a man cast adrift on a desert island.

"I can't see any reason to beat around the bush," Jacobs said to Larry. "I like the script and I want to do the film. How much do you want for it?"

That question was the last thing Larry was expecting to hear, and he almost froze up. "Ah, I let my agent handle that end of it," he said mechanically, taking a quick pull on his drink. The brandy burned his throat and he coughed as he fumbled in his pants pocket for a cigarette.

"Fuck your agent," Jacobs said softly. "I make my deals with the talent. You want to bring him in to draw the contracts, fine. It's you and me that's got to do business."

Cline and Frankel remained silent. Larry looked to his friend for help, but the producer just smiled. "That's a hell of a spot to put me in, Kent." Larry found his voice. "Why don't you just tell me how long an option you had in mind and how much you're willing to pay?"

Jacobs leaned back and grinned. "Ray?"

Cline nodded and looked at Larry's confused expression. "We're not talking options here, DiaMonte," he stated bluntly. "Kent's prepared to drop whatever commitments he can slide out of gracefully and go into principal photography in ninety to one hundred and twenty days." Cline's voice was smooth as a baby's ass. Larry didn't like him already.

Before Cline could elaborate further, Jacobs interrupted. "I don't know you, Larry, but I know your reputation and I like it. I think we could work pretty well together, and you damn well better believe it's gonna be a lot of work." He turned to Cline. "Ray, better give him the bottom line, then get him another drink. I think he's gonna need it."

"We're prepared to offer you three hundred thousand for an outright sale," Cline said.

Larry almost dropped his glass. Then he surprised himself by speaking up. "I couldn't take anything less than four."

Cline narrowed his eyes and began to say something, but Frankel beat him to it. "Are you nuts?"

Jacobs laughed. "He's only joking, Benny." He stared at Larry and his smile was genuine. "Right?"

"I figured one good joke deserved another," Larry

130

sighed.

Cline relaxed and continued, "And you just walk away counting your money. We bring somebody else in for the rewrite. That would, of course, mean sharing screen credit."

Or worse, thought Larry. If whoever did the revision rewrote over two-thirds of the script, Larry could end up with a "story by." Something he was not exactly ecstatic about. No more than he cared to have somebody fucking with his work.

"If you want to be involved in the entire production, and Kent feels you should be, then you get one hundred fifty K up front, against five percent of the total budget." Cline spoke as if he were discussing the odds on a Monday night football game.

Larry did some quick mental calculations. If the film budgeted out at six mil, and that was an absurdly low figure, he'd get his three hundred thou anyway, but it would be longer coming, and he'd earn every damn cent of it.

"And six points in the picture." Jacobs threw out the last bone as if he wasn't sure which direction Larry was leaning.

Larry didn't have to have an abacus to see what that meant. Cline laughed for the first time and said, "From the looks of your expensive taste in ladies, it wouldn't hurt you to be rich."

Jacobs glared at Cline, and the smaller man shut up. Now what the hell was that supposed to mean? But Larry's mind was still in orbit, so he didn't pursue it. "You have just bought yourself a script and a writer, Mr. Jacobs. Now I'll have that other drink, if you don't mind."

Jacobs rose and shook hands with Larry, then went to the bar to refill Larry's glass. He called over one shoulder as he removed the top from a crystal decanter. "We're going to have to go into an extensive rewrite. The part of the police lieutenant, I want it expanded to second lead. I figure the cop can try to determine who's breaking the back of the organization while the lead goes through the main thrust of the story. Kinda have 'em both working toward the same goal, but by different approaches, if you know what I mean."

It wasn't a bad idea, but Larry couldn't see why it was necessary. He said so. "That's going to change the entire tone of the script, Kent. It's just a supporting role. Why build the part?"

Jacobs nodded seriously as he poured brandy into Larry's glass. "Because I'm going to play it."

"You?"

"Somebody's got to hold the horses."

Larry stood up in a state of shock. "Then who the hell is going to play the lead?"

Jacobs grinned like a teenager who just discovered sex and walked to Larry, handing him the glass. "Bethany Drew Jacobs."

Larry sat down hard, emptied the glass, and handed it back. "You're crazy," he said, then wondered if he was, talking to his meal ticket like that.

Jacobs laughed and Frankel broke up. "What's so fucking funny?" Larry demanded.

"That's exactly what she said," Jacobs explained. "Don't you think she can do it?" The film star wasn't laughing now as he looked intently at Larry for a reaction.

Larry just stared vacantly at the far wall. "Christ, I don't know if Mason or Clayburgh could do it. It's not a female role." He spoke softly, as if to himself. "The whole fucking script will have to be rewritten." He paused for a second as his brow knitted. "I guess I could make it her husband that's killed, instead of a kid brother—"

Jacobs broke into Larry's train of thought. "Okay,

132

then, we got a deal. Can't draw the papers till Monday, but if it's all right with you, I'd like you to sit down with Beth and Benny tomorrow, to do the initial run through. Come out in the mornin' and we'll make a day of it. By the time we're finished you should have enough input to start the revision. Whattya say?"

"One hundred and fifty thousand dollars right now?"

"Well, by midweek at the latest."

"What time would you like me to be here tomorrow morning, Mr. Jacobs?"

THIRTEEN

On the way home Larry filled Lynn in on what had transpired in the library without mentioning the amounts involved. "That's fantastic. I'm really happy for you," she said, and he could see that she meant it. "Sounds like you're going to have your hands full for awhile."

"Yeah," Larry grunted. How the hell was he going to keep his ass above swamp water on the show and work on this filmscript revision at the same time? He'd just have to lay off most of *Two Families* on Patte and Lew. They were capable, no doubt about that. He could supervise from the wings and make whatever bone-crushing decisions that were sure to come up. As long as the powers that be didn't see any further lag in the ratings, he'd be home safe.

Larry flirted briefly with the idea of quitting *Two Families Too Many* now that he had some "fuck you" money. It would be nice to take a vacation. He sure the hell deserved it. But he wasn't about to cut off his bread and butter for what could turn out to be Monopoly money. He'd certainly get the hundred and fifty grand. That was a shoo-in, unless Jacobs changed his mind in the next few days—or was hit by a meteor. But Larry had been in the business long enough to know that sometimes even people with the best of intentions didn't get a film in the can. There were more variables involved than a Saturn missile launch, more complications that could prevent a film from going to principal photography, or shut it down before the production was completed, than he cared to think about. It was a crap shoot anyway you figured it. Even if you got it wrapped without any major problems, it could always be shelved for a variety of reasons at the last minute. Maybe he should have just taken the three hundred thousand and run.

"I'd offer you a penny for your thoughts, but the way you look right now, I'm afraid you'd tell me to stick it in my ear." Lynn broke into his reverie.

"Yeah, well, just trying to figure out if I should order the fifty-foot yacht before I know how deep the ocean is."

"Remember what Uncle Fred always said?"

"The scrap merchant?"

"Right. It ain't whats you do, fella, it's hows you do it."

Larry didn't bother stopping in her driveway, he just pulled into his garage and pressed the door close switch on the dashboard. Lynn spoke as he killed the engine. "I don't even get a choice, huh?"

"What? Oh, I figured you'd want to come in for a nightcap."

"A short one."

Larry leered at her as he followed her inside. He flipped the stereo to an FM station as she removed a pair of large circle earrings and set them on one of his keg end tables. "What would you like?"

"You have any orange juice?"

"I think so. Screwdriver?"

"Straight."

He went in to the kitchen and filled a large bubble wine glass with juice and got himself a beer. Back on the sofa he handed her the glass and said, "Here's to sugar on your strawberries."

"Huh?"

Now why had he used that toast? It was one of Flash's favorites from an old Lancaster movie. What was it? Yeah. *The Swimmer*. It was about some crazy dude who swims across town from pool to pool. Sounded like the story of Larry's life. "Nothing, cheers." He leaned back and watched her sip the juice.

She met his gaze and said, "You should really be happy about tonight."

"I am. This is my happy face."

"I'd hate to see the other one." She put her glass down on the table. "What do you want out of life?"

"You ask the hard ones first, huh? Christ, I dunno. Let's see. I got it, four things."

"What?"

"Well, I want to win an Academy Award for best screenplay, I'd like to write the Great American Novel some day, I want to make love to you again." He went on quickly, before she could react, "And, oh yeah, I'd like to see the island of Crete someday."

"Why Crete?"

"'Cause it was the first thing that came to mind for number four when I was trying to slide number three by you."

She laughed and shook her head. "Did you think I wouldn't catch it?"

"I figured if I ran it by you fast enough it would only register subliminally. You know, like a posthypnotic suggestion. In about ten minutes you'd attack me and I'd have to fight for my honor again."

"Is that what you really want?"

Larry reached into his back pocket and removed a folded white handkerchief and waved it in her face. They both laughed, then Lynn's smile dissolved. "I'm sorry that happened."

"I'm not."

136

"It isn't going to happen again," she stated firmly.

"I don't understand you, Singer. I thought it was pretty good—for both of us."

"I'm sorry I gave you the impression we were going to sleep together again. I didn't mean to. I was just having such a good time I didn't want the evening to end. I think I'd better go now," she said formally as she rose.

"Aw, come one. For the first time in months I got something to celebrate. Least you could do is stick around for a while."

"Congratulations. I wish you all the success you can handle," she said, as she opened the front door.

Larry took her in his arms and kissed her lightly. She didn't respond. "If you change your mind, just pound on the wall."

She smiled sadly. "I'll remember that. Goodnight." He stood there, watching her go down the walkway until she disappeared around the corner of the garage. Then he shut the door and went back to the sofa. He sat there for several minutes drinking his beer and trying to determine what she was all stirred up about. Go figure women.

As he got up to get himself another beer he passed the guest bath. Her clothing was still hanging over the sink. He scooped it into a bundle and ran for the door.

He was clutching her dress under one arm, a bra, and a pair of black silk panties draped over his elbow as he opened the door with his free hand.

"I always said you were psychic." He almost collapsed from the shock of seeing Patte Gordon standing nose to nose with him, her finger poised over the doorbell.

She was wearing tight faded jeans, a cowboy shirt, and Western boots. "You scared the hell out of me, Flash."

Patte stared at the lingerie, then squinted at him. "She must have either left in one hell of a hurry, or your taste in clothing is as kinky as I always thought it was."

Larry laughed and stepped back to let her enter. "Would you believe there's an invisible woman running around out there looking for Claude Rains?"

"Sure, but I'd believe anything. For a while there I was even convinced you were a broken-hearted friend who needed some moral support to get through these trying times. I can see I underestimated your recuperative powers."

Larry dropped the clothing on a chair and led her to the sofa, ignoring the remark. "What brings you out this way?"

Patte looked surprised. "I'm here for the meeting. Didn't Lew get hold of you?"

"What are you talking about?"

"There's a big problem with next week's taping. Ned Vickers and Lew should be here any minute with some company lawyers and a couple of network heavies. Don't tell me nobody got through to you? Hell, I must have left five messages on your machine myself."

Larry blanched and sat down hard. "Ah, I haven't checked my messages yet. What kind of problem?" He asked the question, but he really didn't want to hear the answer.

"Mitchell Donovan was arrested for child molestation at six o'clock this evening," she said evenly. "He's being held at L.A. County on one million dollars bail."

Larry's eyes widened. "Oh, shit! A million bucks? Who the fuck did he molest?"

"Me."

Larry looked at her serious expression for a second, then she burst into a fit of hysterical laughter, fell over on her side, and buried her face in the sofa cushions. Larry's jaw tightened. "You bitch." He picked up a loose throw pillow and hit her with it. She tried to scoot away but he was too fast for her. He tackled her and brought her to the floor, pinning her body beneath his.

"That wasn't fair," he growled, as she tried to squirm out of his grasp. He noticed that she wasn't trying all that hard.

"Sure it was. You were standing there with your hands full of underwear, looking like you were king of the world. You were so self-satisfied you almost made me barf," she panted. "Now, get off my chest so I can breathe—or get serious."

Larry blushed and sat back against the sofa. "That was a dirty trick, Gordon. I'll get you for that one."

Patte leaned on one elbow and grinned. "Promise?"

"So what do you want, you should excuse the expression?"

Patte straightened her shirt. "Just wanted to see how you were. I was out at the Saddle Horn with some friends—"

"The what?"

"It's a new Country-Western place off Roscoe in Panorama City."

"Somehow I don't see you doing the Okie stomp to shit-kicking music."

"It's my second most favorite thing."

"Uh-uh. I'm not going to walk into that one. It is nice to see you, though."

"And you, sir, are looking much better than the last time I saw you."

Larry smiled. "Lady, you ain't heard nothing yet. Just sit there and prepare yourself for the weirdest story since *Dog Day Afternoon*." He began by showing her the kidney stone. She was properly impressed, but her eyes widened and her mouth fell open when he launched into the details of the meeting at the Jacobs house.

When he finished she expelled a deep breath and said, "Now you're putting me on."

139

"Nope. Everything I told you was gospel truth, uninterrupted by commercial messages, and just about the best thing that's happened to me since Hillary Langendorf."

"Who?"

"She was sixteen and I was seventeen. We were at a drive-in movie in the back seat of my 'Forty-two Plymouth on New Year's Eve, during my senior year in high school. The film was some oater, I can't remember—some slow-moving love story with Gary Cooper—"

"*The Cowboy and the Lady*; Cooper, Merle Oberon, and Walter Brennan; 1939. You were probably watching the first run."

"Very funny, Flash. Anyway, we were humping away like two monkeys in heat—"

"And you asked her if she wanted to do it dog-fashion and she said, 'Yeah, you sniff and I'll growl.'"

"Why don't I just lean back and let you finish the story?"

Patte looked properly chastised, so Larry continued. "There we were, oblivious to all, when suddenly the lights came up and a fireworks display erupts over our heads. It was midnight and we were so involved we had lost all track of time. I'm telling you, Flash, you haven't made it till you've gotten off under the rockets' red glare."

"Spare me the *glory* details, DiaMonte." Patte scowled.

Larry groaned then punched her playfully on the shoulder. "So what do you think? Am I going to be a big time screenwriter or what?"

"I think you could be anything you wanted to," Patte said seriously. "If you wanted it badly enough. I've always admired your ability to persevere." She nodded at Lynn's clothing. "Even under the most adverse conditions." Then she took his hand. "I'm really happy for you." She lowered her eyes and spoke softly. "There is one thing you can do for me."

"Name it."

140

She went into a provocative pose, one hand fluffing her hair as she batted her lashes. "Ah'd do just anythin' for a part in your picture, Mistah DiaMonte, suh."

They both laughed and Larry got to his feet. "Hey, you hungry?"

"Starving. Whatcha got in mind?" she leered.

"Eggs," Larry said, as she followed him into the kitchen. Patte beat him to the refrigerator door and opened it. "My God," she exclaimed. "It's all beer."

Larry pointed to the two door shelves full of eggs. Patte took four off the top shelf. "Use the ones on the bottom, they're older."

"Why don't you number them?"

"I did, but the ink keeps coming off every time I wash them."

Patte cooked up two large omelettes while Larry opened a bottle of Chateau Pichon Lalande, '73. They ate at the coffee table after Larry had tossed a couple of logs in the fireplace. They finished the bottle with their meal and Larry said, "I can open another one, unless you have to run off?"

He was halfway to the bar when she replied, "I can stay as long as you want me to."

"Great," he called back, either not hearing the inference in her tone—or ignoring it.

They sat in front of the fire for two hours, Larry doing most of the talking. He described animatedly what he planned for the revised version of *Five'll Get You Ten,* and Patte listened intently, commenting now and then, and laughing often enough to let him know she appreciated the black humor that riddled the script like holes in a pair of bachelor's socks.

Finally, Larry paused for breath and looked at the clock. "Jesus, how time flies when you're extolling your own virtues." He yawned. "We'd both better call it a night or

141

we're going to be useless tomorrow."

Patte got up and stretched. "Yeah, you're absolutely right." She turned on her heel and headed for the entry hall. Larry was about to comment on the abruptness of her departure, but instead his mouth fell open as she began climbing the stairs to the bedroom.

PART THREE

QB VII and a Half

FOURTEEN

Even to a man who was used to high-pressure situations and frenetic scrambling, the next two weeks resembled a Chinese fire drill choreographed by the Marx Brothers. Not that Larry was complaining. It kept his mind off other things, namely Robyn, Lynn, Flash, and his kids.

He had driven out to the Jacobs place the morning after Patte had spent the night at his house. Kent, Bethany, and Frankel had been lounging at the pool when he arrived. They were all in bathing suits, and once again Larry felt like an intruder. Beth noticed his nervousness and dragged him off to the pool house where he selected a suit, then rejoined the others at the pool.

Kent did most of the talking while Larry made extensive notes in the script margins. Bethany interrupted occasionally with comments that surprised Larry. Contrary to what some of her public thought, she was definitely a pro, and her advice, for the most part, was sound and creative. She knew better than any of them how difficult the role was, and she alone knew if she could pull it off.

Kent was absolutely certain she could do it, and with style. Frankel was reserved and Larry could see that the producer shared some of his own doubts. But as the morning wore on Larry's misgivings were beginning to fade. The lady knew her craft and her husband was no slouch either. Just maybe she'd be able to deliver a performance that would blow the doors off every theater in the country. Maybe.

"Now, we got the Caddy limo in hot pursuit of Beth's car," Kent said, as he turned a page. "I think we ought to insert a little comedy relief right about there. Maybe Beth drives through a flower stand or jumps a curb and narrowly misses something. I don't know. I just don't want it to get too heavy there. Whatta ya think?"

Larry sighed deeply. "I'm talking about a film like *No Way to Treat a Lady* and—"

"Which would have been an excellent title for this one," Frankel chimed in.

Larry gave him a dirty look and continued. "You're giving me *Smokey and the Bandit Go to Morocco*. No way."

"Well, I'll go along with that," Kent seemed to acquiesce.

"Good."

"After you convince me."

Larry frowned. "Okay, the worst thing we can do is slapstick this thing up. You want funny there? Then we give Beth a line. Or better yet, her car screeches to a corner, she slows enough to take it without tipping over, and as she cramps the wheel with one hand, she sticks the other one out the window, making a right turn signal, then with her hand in the air, extends her middle finger."

Beth laughed. Kent nodded. "Not bad. Not fantastic, but not bad."

"What I'm saying is that's an option. We got a high-tension moment there, and I agree, we should lighten it up a little. I'll come up with something that'll work, but let's lose the flower stand, okay?"

"Okay. Just don't disappoint me," Kent said.

"Have I ever?" Larry replied.

Kent chuckled and shook his head, and Larry was sure he was wondering about the sanity of writers in general.

By two o'clock, Larry had covered sixty script pages with notes and he was beginning to feel weak from hunger. During the long morning session Bethany and Kent had acknowledged his expertise in a number of areas, and he was forced to do the same when they convinced him he was wrong. But that was the way a good script was born, he knew, and so far he felt comfortable with the changes.

Frankel had wandered off to a bar that had been set up near the French doors that led to the library, and Bethany was floating in a pool chair, a glass of tomato juice in her hand. Kent pressed a button on the base of a telephone on the umbrella table at his side and a male servant appeared from the house. "Art, I think it's about time we fed these good people. I'll have a T-bone and salad. Larry?"

"Ah, yeah, sounds good to me."

Kent turned to the pool. "The usual, hon?"

"No," Bethany called back. "Just some cottage cheese and pineapple."

Kent addressed the servant. "Bring Mrs. Jacobs's cottage cheese and a quarter-pound of ground sirloin, medium." He smiled at his wife. "You're gonna need all your strength, Slick."

Larry groaned inwardly. It looked like it was going to be a long day.

They all sat around the table, while three servants laid out the lunch. Frankel had ordered lox, onion rolls, and cream cheese, and Larry wondered how anybody could eat like that in the middle of the day. Three different bottles of wine were opened, with names Larry had never heard before, but were nevertheless admirable, he had to admit.

147

Frankel did most of the talking while the others ate. "There's not a lot we can do until we get the first draft of the new script. I've got a pretty good idea what it'll cost out at just from reading the original and listening to today's changes. But we can't go to budget until we have all the pages. Larry, what kind of time table are you looking at?"

Larry put down the piece of steak he was about to fork into his mouth. "If we get through the whole script today, I can have the revision in, say, two weeks." If I don't eat, sleep, or move at less than Mach two, he added to himself.

"Sounds good to me," Kent said. "Beth and Benny and me'll work on casting in the meantime. I got some good old boys in mind that I think'll really enjoy this one. Once we're all satisfied with this draft you won't be seein' much of me. I've got to wrap up some business in Atlanta, so you'll be dealin' directly with Benny or Beth."

Frankel had explained to Larry earlier that the film was to be a joint project of RedEye and Jacobs's own company, JayDee Films. It was to be produced under the masthead of "5/10" Productions, with Frankel as producer and Kent as exec. Frankel was to be the ramrod that saw to it everything went according to plan and that the film was brought in on time and—hopefully—not disastrously over budget. Kent and Bethany were doing the film without salary, but of course they owned most of the picture. Kent hoped to sell it to a big studio for distribution before it was wrapped, which was usually the way he did business with a film of his own. Larry knew that was the way to go. If the picture cost eight mil to make and they got four from UA or somebody for distribution rights, that would put them that much closer to the twenty-four million earn-out figure the film would need to start showing a profit—for Larry anyway.

No director had been discussed, and Larry found that a

148

bit strange. Besides the writer, he felt that was the most important job on the film. It was almost imperative that a director be involved in the initial concepts they were hammering out today. Problems were bound to come up when the director wanted to throw his two cents in and Larry could see some unavoidable delays in the near future. So he brought it up over dessert.

"Didn't I tell you?" Kent grinned. "I'm going to direct."

Larry narrowed his eyes and leaned forward and across the table. "You got any more surprises for me, superstar? You're not going to be first cameraman, key grip, or script girl too, are you?"

"Shit. If it'd make it a better film, you bet your belt buckle."

Larry had come to like Kent in the short time he had known him personally. He had a laid-back, low-profile attitude that was disarming. He used that slow talking, country-boy drawl to mask what Larry was beginning to see as a brilliant mind. "If that's the case, I got a request."

"You name it," Kent said.

"I want a part in the picture."

Jacobs began to laugh uproariously. Bethany gave Larry a right-on nod, and Frankel stuck a piece of salmon in his mouth. "You're kiddin'," Kent said, as he calmed down.

"Nope. If Dickey and Benchley can do it, by God, so can DiaMonte."

"Gratis?" Kent asked.

"Scale," Larry demanded.

Kent turned to Bethany. "Christ, we're working for nothin' and *he* wants to get paid!"

"You know in the mortuary scene?" Beth asked Kent, who nodded. "He can play the third corpse from the left."

Frankel almost choked on his roll. Before Larry could protest, Kent said, "Naw, I've always been against type castin'."

"As the director, I'll leave it to you," Larry said. "Just make sure I don't have to shave my beard."

They worked until dark. By the time Larry left, he had all he needed from the story conference to wade into the revision with both feet, and he was itching to begin.

It had been a grueling fifteen days, but this morning he had sent the final pages over to Frankel's office and he was certain everybody would be overjoyed with his fantastic new script. He had gotten his check last week and he figured, what the hell, if the script was bad enough to detonate underground in Nevada, he was still home free.

Patte and Lew had done yeomen's work on the show and he had managed to cover his long absences because the pages got in on time. Actually, he was surprised that nobody missed him more.

He had dated Lynn several times, taking her to a couple of guild screenings and dinners, but he had been preoccupied with juggling two jobs, and nothing had come of the early evenings.

He had seen very little of Patte since their night together in bed. He leaned back in his chair and lit a cigarette, letting his mind dwell on that evening.

He hadn't really been surprised when Flash trotted upstairs. He had shut off the lights, put the wine bottles in the garbage, and used the downstairs bathroom. By the time he reached the second-floor back bedroom, she was in the king-size water bed, facing the wall with the fur spread tucked up around her shoulders. She looked so damn tiny in that big bed, like a teddy bear somebody had forgotten to put away.

He flipped off the lights and got undressed silently in the moonlight that spilled through the balcony windows. He dropped his clothing on the chaise near the dresser and crawled into bed beside her on his back and waited for the motion of the water to subside. He couldn't figure

150

out what her motives were. Obviously, he was the most desirable male in town, of that he had no doubt. Then the thought struck him that maybe she was just as lonely as he had been until he met Lynn.

As his eyes became accustomed to the semidarkness, he studied her bare shoulder, stark white against the darkness of the bedspread. As he watched, she turned over on her back and the cover fell away exposing her breasts. They were larger than he had thought, looking firm and inviting, their wide button nipples pointing toward the ceiling.

He reached over and carefully slipped the cover downward, exposing her long narrow waist and the shapely curve of her hips. She shivered and her entire body undulated quietly. Before he could finish categorizing her assets with his eyes, he had a full erection, one of the best he ever had. He always felt that way when he made love to a woman for the first time. It was going to be a memorable night, he decided.

Reaching down with one hand, Patte grabbed at the covers and pulled them up to her chin, mumbled something he couldn't make out, and curled her body into a fetal position, facing the wall again.

She was sound asleep. So much for the well-laid plans of mice and writers. Aw, tell me about the farm and the beavers again, George, Larry felt like saying aloud, but he just rolled over and punched his pillow.

The next morning when he woke up, he was alone in the bed. Downstairs he found a note taped to his typewriter:

YOU WERE ABSOLUTELY FANTASTIC
LAST NIGHT. NEXT TIME, I'LL
BRING THE ROMAN CANDLES.

HILLARY LANGENDORF

Larry had a half-gallon *Jack Daniels Maxwell House* bottle filled with pennies on his mantlepiece. He had won the booze as a door prize at his twenty-year high-school reunion six years ago. After the liquor was gone, which he recalled had been about two weeks later, he had started throwing coins into the bottle, and now it was damn near full. He had been using it as an ornate bookend since he moved into his new place.

He went to the second-floor landing and picked up a wicker basket that held a half dead spider plant. Dumping the dirt into the sink, plant and all, he shook out the basket and filled it to the brim with the pennies from the bottle. Setting it in the corner of his desk top he stuck the carbon-steel carnation into the copper soil and stood back to admire his handiwork. Then he took a business card and printed in large block letters on its reverse: WATER TWICE MONTHLY WITH THREE-IN-ONE OIL, and propped the card at the base of the flower.

When he had glanced at the flower again in the morning, it seemed to be surviving the transplant nicely.

But now he was done. The script would stand or fall on its own merits, and it would be weeks until he would be further involved in the film. *Two Families* was moving along steadily, the Christmas show due to air on two consecutive Monday nights before December twenty-fifth. He felt like partying. Today was his forty-first birthday. He had gotten a card from his sons yesterday, and he might even call and thank them. Patte didn't mention the fact that he was a year older, and he wasn't sure she knew today was the big day. He had refrained from telling Lynn because he didn't want her to make a fuss. Well, he *did* want her to make a fuss, but he couldn't figure out a way to bring the subject up in casual conversation. He had all day to work on that one.

Larry sat alone in the office. Lew was out on the set

somewhere and Patte hadn't come in yet. The phone on his desk rang. It was his late female coworker. "Good morning," she said. "Working hard?'"

"Harder than you. When you coming in?"

"I've been in for the last hour. I've been out on the set since eight. Vickers buttonholed me on the way in. He's got a problem. You better get out here right away."

Larry hung up and left the office. He walked across the large lot to the sound stage. It was nearly deserted and Vickers stood scowling at Patte in front of the duplex set as he approached. They were standing almost inside the cutaway top floor. They seemed to be arguing. A couple of camera people were covering their equipment and none of the cast was present. It looked as if they had shut down the shooting for the day. That's all he needed.

"What's wrong?" Larry asked, as he joined them.

"You're not going to believe this," Vickers said, as he tugged nervously on the stopwatch cord around his neck. "You got to see it for yourself." He led Larry around the side of the set to the open area that was the driveways and astroturf front lawns of the duplex. Patte fell in behind them, trailing by a few feet and looking grim. Larry should have figured it out, but he didn't. He walked right into it.

At least a hundred people shouted, "Surprise!" and he almost cashed in right there. Two long tables were set up in the nearest driveway. They were heavily laden with booze and a large cake with "Writers Are People Too. So Are Axe Murderers and Rapists" written across it in black icing.

The entire cast was present, along with all the crew. Patte and Vickers laughed as they all mobbed him, punching him on the back and making crude jokes about his age. Before the crowd could hoist him on their shoulders and break into a chorus of "For He's a Jolly Good Fellow," Patte climbed up on a chair and yelled for attention. It took a full minute before the group calmed down enough to hear her. "Mr. Big Time Writer," she said ceremoniously. "We, all the little people that have contributed to your success in some small way, would like to wish you a happy birthday and let you know that even though you thought you finally made the grade, it's all up hill from here."

The applause was deafening and Madeline, who had donned a skimpy maid's costume from wardrobe, fought her way into the crowd, carrying a large tray covered with champagne glasses. Mitchell Donovan grabbed two glasses from the tray and elbowed his way through the mass of bodies to Larry's side. "Don't pay any attention to Gordon," he said, as he handed Larry a glass. "She thinks she's funny."

"I hope so," Larry said, as he sipped the champagne.

Donovan laughed. "No, I mean we all owe you a lot, even if we don't let you know that sometimes."

Larry looked at Donovan closely. "Why thank you, Mitch. I appreciate that."

"*De nada*. Can I get you something to eat?"

"What do you want now, Mitch?"

Donovan assumed a shocked expression. "Me?" I just wanted to wish you a happy birthday."

"Okay, I'll buy that."

"But now that you mentioned it, you know the bit in the Christmas special where I disguise myself as Santa Claus and pretend to come down Karen's chimney?"

"Yeah, Mitch," Larry said warily.

"Something's wrong with the dialogue there."

"Jesus, Donovan, it's already in the can!"

"We could reshoot that one scene easy enough. You know, where I say, 'Ho, Ho'? I think there should be three Ho's there." Before he could react, Donovan broke into a fit of laughter and grabbed Larry around the neck and

154

kissed him on the cheek. "Happy birthday, Lar."

Donovan moved away as Larry was congratulated by the rest of the cast. He felt good. It was nice to be among friends he loved. Patte stood to one side of the long tables, looking at her watch, and Larry noticed the concern on her face. He disengaged from his wellwishers and went to her side, pulling her away from the mob who were beginning to sing old ribald Army ballads. "Got a date?" he asked her, nodding at her watch.

"Nope. Got two birthday presents for you." She opened her large purse and removed a manila envelope and handed it to him. He smiled and tore the flap, reached in and took out a garish bumper sticker that read: SAGIT-TARIANS MAKE BETTER LOVERS.

"You know I don't put stickers on my car," he said, as he hugged her.

"Just wet it and plaster it across your ass. Then every time you drop your pants, you get free advertising."

"What's the other present?" he said, leering. "You answer the ad?"

She took his hand and drew away from the party to the side door of the sound stage. Outside in the parking lot Lew was leaning against the side of his van looking like he had just been promoted to head of the network. "What the hell's going on?" Larry asked. Patte smiled and walked to the side of the van and slid open the long door. Steve and L.J. jumped to the ground, shouting, and tackled Larry. When he managed to recover he had one boy under each arm and tears in his eyes. He looked at Patte. "How did you manage this?" he said, his voice choking up.

"Don't say anything, just go spend the rest of the day with your kids."

He let go of the boys and hugged her mightily, then kissed her on the forehead. "You're all right, Flash, you know that?" he said, as he dabbed at the moisture on his cheeks.

"I just came up with the idea. Robyn was the one who agreed. Maybe you ought to thank her." She pushed him away. "Now get the hell out of here before some real emergency comes up."

FIFTEEN

Larry got in behind the wheel of the Porsche and Steve scrunched into the passenger seat with his younger brother on his lap. L.J. had a package in his hands which he was clutching tightly. "What's that?" Larry asked.

It's your birthday present," L.J. grinned broadly. "Steve paid for it with his own money, but I picked it out."

Larry started the car and edged out of the parking lot. "When do you guys have to be home?" he inquired casually.

"Mom said by dinner time," Steve replied. "Mom and her friend are going to take us out to—"

Larry gunned the car down the street. "I don't want to hear about your mother's friend," he growled.

They drove in uncomfortable silence for a few blocks, then L.J. spoke up. "Where we goin', Dad?"

"I want to show you where I live now. And there's somebody I want you to meet."

When they arrived at Larry's town house, the two kids walked around gawking and exploring every corner while Larry phoned Lynn. She was home asleep, and he apologized for waking her. After he explained he had two miniature DiaMontes he wanted her to meet she agreed to dress and come over.

157

Larry let her in a few minutes later and introduced her to the boys. She bubbled over them and Steve quieted down and sat withdrawn in one corner of the sofa. L.J. didn't seem to be affected as much by the beautiful lady, and he launched into a description of his latest acquisition, a pool table that had been given him by his mother's boyfriend.

Larry winced and stared at the painting. Then he felt like laughing. She hated pool tables. Full circle.

Lynn caught the look of pain on his face and changed the subject. "What's in the box, goose?" she said, as she poked L.J. playfully in the stomach.

He fell back on the couch laughing. "It's Dad's birthday present."

Lynn glared at Larry. "You didn't tell me it was your birthday."

"Yeah, well, musta slipped my mind."

"Let's open it!" L.J. yelled, and grabbed the paper-wrapped box. He began to tear away the ribbon.

"Whoa, there. I thought it was your Dad's gift," Lynn chuckled.

"That's okay. He always opens my presents. Sometimes at Christmas I wonder why they bother to have me around at all." Larry stopped before he could feel any sorrier for himself and ruin the moment.

L.J. attacked the paper like Jack the Ripper on a particularly violent night, and Steve perked up a bit as his brother pulled the lid from the box.

It was a cashmere sweater, very yellow and very expensive. Larry doubted seriously if Steve had sprung for it himself. He lifted it out of the box and ran his hand over the soft material. Now why would Rob even care? Then he began to laugh.

"What's so funny?" Lynn asked.

"It's the same sweater that Alda wore in *California*

Suite." He held it up to his chest. "I do bear a striking resemblance, don't I?"

"Does she look like Jane Fonda?" Lynn said softly.

Larry grabbed the kids and kissed them. "I can't remember."

They sang happy birthday to him, then Larry excused himself and went upstairs. He removed his slacks and tossed them into a corner. Taking a pair of white yachting pants from the closet he put them on, then pulled the sweater over his head. Kicking off his shoes, he replaced them with a pair of white golf sneakers and stood looking at himself in the full-length mirror. He ran a hand through his hair and nodded at his reflection. "Why not?" he said aloud.

As he came down the stairs L.J. jumped up. "Dad, I'm hungry. Let's go to MacDonalds."

"How about a nice restaurant? We can all have a good meal and talk," Larry said as he picked the boy up and hoisted him over his head.

"I want to go to MacDonalds, then roller skating," L.J. protested. "I want to show you how good I can skate now."

Larry put him down and turned to Steve. "What do you want to do?"

"Don't make no difference to me. Whatever the shrimp wants is okay."

"Looks like you're outnumbered," Lynn said.

"How do you figure that? I've got your vote, don't I?"

"Hell no, I want to go roller skating too."

They took Lynn's car and Larry drove. Lynn leaned over the seat and engaged the boys in conversation about their schoolwork, trying to draw Steve into the discussion. The morose teenager just grunted and nodded occasionally,

159

and Larry could see he was in one of his moods. He turned slightly in the driver's seat and said, "How would you like to meet Bethany Drew?"

Steve's eyes lit up like a pinball machine. "When?"

"Oh, I don't know. Maybe next time I go out to their house I could take you with me. You could go swimming while we talk business. I mean, if you're interested in going."

"All right!" the two boys yelled in unison. Then Steve asked, "How'd you get to meet her?"

"She and her husband are doing a movie I wrote," Larry said offhandedly, as if it were the kind of thing that occurred daily. The kids had been on the *Two Families* set often enough and they had met the cast, so they weren't easily impressed with the glitter end of the business. But Steve had one of Bethany's famous posters on his bedroom wall, and L.J. had been a fan of Kent's for a long time.

Lynn relaxed back against the headrest and winked at Larry, as if to say, You just pushed the right button, my friend.

"A TV movie?" Steve asked suspiciously.

"A theatrical film, m'boy. The kind you have to pay five bucks a pop to see." He grinned into the rearview mirror. "But if you stay on the good side of your old man, I might just be able to get you into the premiere.

"Free?" L.J. asked seriously.

They all laughed, even Steve.

By the time they reached MacDonalds, Larry had explained the details of the film sale as the boys listened intently. Steve even asked questions about production schedules and casting that Larry answered as best he could. Even though Steve was damn near as tall as he was, and L.J. was growing like a St. Bernard puppy, Larry knew that when he accepted the Oscar for best script these were the little people he was going to thank. No matter how you cut it, making movies was a hell of a lot more interesting to kids than selling real estate.

After they had all stuffed themselves with Big Macs and fries, Lynn surprising Larry by wading in like a hungry hobo, they drove to a nearby rink. Larry hadn't been inside one since he was a kid, and the disco atmosphere was distracting. It was the middle of the day, but the place was packed. The boys donned rented skates and rolled out into the jam of swaying bodies under the swirling multicolored lights, while Larry sat on a bench beside Lynn and laced his skates.

"I promised myself I'm not going to fall down on the rink and embarrass everybody. You hold on tight and maybe together we can pull it off."

Lynn took his arm and they plodded across the rug to the single step that led up to the polished hardwood floor. Larry kept his promise; he didn't fall down on the rink. He fell flat on his ass trying to maneuver the low step.

They spent the next two hours with Lynn acting as a human crutch and Larry skating like a man with two left legs. They laughed a lot, and although Larry's balance improved as the afternoon wore on, he didn't let it show, holding on to her much more than necessary. The two boys darted around them like World War II fighter planes engaged in a running dogfight, Steve trying to act casual and L.J. grinning from ear to ear.

Afterward they went into the adjoining arcade and Larry broke a twenty and filled the kids' hands with coins. He and Lynn walked around, playing an occasional game, competing with each other on the Submarine Hunt and anything else two people could play. He won most of the time. He wondered if she were trying very hard.

On the way home, L.J., stuffed to the gills with candy and junk food, fell asleep in Lynn's lap. Steve lounged

161

alone in the back seat staring out the window. Lynn ran her hand through L.J.'s mop of hair and said, "This one's not going to be in any condition to go out to a big dinner with his mother."

"Yeah," Larry smiled evilly. "Too bad, huh?"

"You're a horrid person, you know that?"

"Who, me?" Larry asked innocently and they both laughed.

Larry pulled into the driveway of his old home and parked beside the ever-present Jag sedan. His good humor quickly ebbed as he shut off the engine. Lynn woke L.J. and helped him out of the car. It was still light, and Larry could see Robyn standing at the front window peering out at them. Lynn was on the side of the car closest to the house. He knew Robyn was getting a good look at her. That small triumph made him feel a little better.

He hugged and kissed the boys and watched them walk to the front door. Then he and Lynn settled back into the BMW and pulled away.

"All of a sudden you look like you just lost your best friend. Was it because you had to say goodbye to your sons?" Lynn asked sympathetically.

"Naw, it's my wife's boyfriend. I feel like strangling that son of a bitch most of the time."

"Very unhealthy attitude. You've got to let go of that, my friend."

"You know that and I know that, but try telling it to my twisted subconscious."

"Seems to me that if she's the bitch you claim she is, and he's a loser too, then they deserve each other. You're the one that wins."

Larry considered her statement. She was absolutely right. He was far better off. Why, then, did it still feel like a no-win situation? "It just galls the hell out of me to see him

162

taking over my house and my kids. Robyn never disciplined those two, that was always my job. I'm sure she hasn't changed, and you can bet your ass *he* doesn't give 'em so much as a harsh look. So everything's dandy, and ole Dad comes off looking like a blackguard." Larry shifted violently as he pulled out of a stop light on Devonshire. Every time he thought about it he came close to flying into a blind rage.

"It's about time you sold that horse," Lynn said pointedly.

"What?"

"You're like a thoroughbred owner. You raised the animal, trained it, and groomed it. You strut around like a peacock displaying it, and when it wins a race, you give it a lump of sugar and take all the credit. You didn't really love the horse, but it was your property and you owned it. When somebody came along and rustled it, you became the victim of the grossest injustice of all time. Forget about that mare, there's plenty of fillies out there." She paused and looked over at him. "A fact I think you're already aware of."

"My, don't we wax philosophical? You have any more little axioms you want to lay on me?"

Lynn punched him on the shoulder and said, "To put it in a language you can understand, Mr. DiaMonte, fuck all of them but six. Save them for pallbearers."

Larry damn near lost control of the car. When he had the BMW back in its proper lane and the tears of laughter wiped away from his eyes, he said, "Maybe you should be the writer and I should be the beautiful lady."

She reached over and took his hand. "I kind of like it this way."

Larry pulled into her driveway, got out and opened her door and handed her the keys. "Why don't we change and head for the beach?"

163

Lynn frowned. "Sorry, I've got a date."

Larry looked crushed. She moved into his arms and kissed him warmly. "How about tomorrow night?"

"I don't know," he pouted. "I may have to go down to the paddock to look over the new arrivals."

"Well, I'll keep it open anyway. You call me."

"Hey, I've been meaning to ask. Had you met Ray Cline before the other night?"

"Why?" She was immediately on the defensive and Larry could have kicked himself for butting into what was none of his business.

"Just wondered." Larry leaned on the side of the car and avoided her gaze. "It looked like you two might have known each other."

"Our paths may have crossed somewhere. It's not that big a town."

Only eight or so million people, thought Larry. Not much bigger than Upper Cut, Nebraska.

"Did he say something?" Lynn seemed to be giving it more interest than it deserved.

"No, it was nothing. Goodnight, lady. Take care, huh?"

She nodded and walked to her door. Larry couldn't help noticing the look of apprehension on her face.

SIXTEEN

It was a wonderful day. All was right with the world. Larry had called Lynn the next evening and they had gone out together several times in the last week. The subject of sex hadn't come up, but Larry was confident all she needed was a little romancing and he'd have her back in the sack in no time.

He came into the office early, whistling, a smile etched permanently into his features. It was good to be alive, everything was going his way, and he hadn't even thought about Robyn recently, other than considering proposing a truce. Even she didn't look so bad today. Maybe he'd be his usual magnanimous self and call her about some bilateral peace talks.

Lew was hunched over his typewriter, pounding away, and he acknowledged Larry's cheery greeting with a passing grunt. Patte was working on the *Variety* crossword puzzle. "Need a three-letter word for humorist," she said, as he fell into his big swivel chair and put his feet up on the desk.

"What *you* are half of, my dear Gordon. Wit." Larry placed his hands behind his head and stared at the ceiling with a preoccupied expression on his face.

"Hey, you're getting better," Patte smiled.

"That's what she said." Larry nodded.

"Will you two shut the hell up?" Lew called across the room. "I'm trying to work here."

Patte scowled and put the paper down. "What's the hardnose working on this morning?" Larry asked her.

"His doctoral thesis. He's doing a paper on the effects of comedy writing during the Spanish Inquisition. He's calling it 'Laugh till it hurts.'"

"That's bad, Flash."

"It's early yet. I get badder. Oh, Ray Cline called just before you came in." She did a good imitation of Cline's nasal twang. "Wants you to call him ASAP."

Larry sat up and grabbed the phone. "Thanks."

When he got Cline on the line, the business manager told him he had heard from Kent and Bethany last night. They had both read the first draft revision and they were ecstatic. "I got to hand it to you, DiaMonte, you came through like a real professional. Frankly, I was never really crazy about the project to begin with."

Larry hadn't been exactly sure why he disliked Cline, but he was beginning to get some idea. Cline went on, "They left for Mazatlan for a week, but they'll be wanting to meet with you as soon as they get back. Be available."

"That's me. Everready Larry. Just let me know where and when."

"How was the lady that night, pal?"

"Whattaya mean?"

Cline laughed. "You know damn well what I mean, DiaMonte. Did you get your money's worth?"

Larry's hand clenched the receiver. "I don't know what you're talking about."

Patte looked up from her puzzle and saw Larry's face whiten. "All right, play it your way," Cline said. "But next time, have a little more class, huh? Kent was too much of a gentleman to say anything, but shit, bringing somebody

166

like that into his home. You got balls, I got to give you that." Cline hung up, and Larry sat there with the phone in his hand.

"Bad news?" Patte asked, as she got up and sat on the edge of his desk.

"Huh?"

"I said, did they decide to make your film into an animated cartoon, with you playing the lead?"

"Oh, no, everything's fine . . ."

"It don't look fine. Want to tell old Flash about it?"

Before Larry could reply the door opened and Ned Vickers stood there, looking unhappier than usual. "I want to see you now, DiaMonte. In my office." He turned on his heel and without waiting for an answer, stalked off.

"Oh oh," Patte said. "He looks like Alec Guinness in *Tunes of Glory,* when he found out he was getting a new C.O."

Larry rose and walked out without commenting. What the hell was Cline trying to say? If the man was trying to irritate him, he was sure succeeding. Larry walked down the long hall and entered Vickers's outer office. The inner door was open and the producer was sitting formally behind his desk. Larry didn't like the look on his face.

A thin man in a business suit was standing beside the desk and Larry didn't see him until he was well inside the office. "Mr. Lawrence DiaMonte?"

"Yes?" Larry answered in confusion.

The man opened his briefcase and removed a folded sheaf of paper wrapped in a blue cover and handed it to Larry. It was a summons.

The man snapped his briefcase closed with a gesture of finality. "Thank you, Mr. Vickers, Mr. DiaMonte." He walked around Larry who stood there like a statue, and left the office.

Larry came out of his trance and waved the papers at

167

Vickers. "What the hell's this?"

"Sit down."

Larry perched on the edge of one of the chairs in front of the desk and tapped the folder nervously in his hand. Vickers sighed and said, "That, my friend, is a two million dollar law suit. Now, that may not sound like big money to you since you got a part-time job, but frankly, it's got me and the people at the network kinda concerned."

Larry pulled open the folder and scanned the first page: "Robyn DiaMonte" "libel" "defamation of character" "public ridicule" "loss of business" "damage to reputation." The words glowed on the page like a neon sign. "Jesus Christ!" Larry moaned.

"As a matter of fact, those were Bill Foy's exact words." Foy was the president of the network and Larry had only met him once, but he could understand his reaction. "Personally, I don't think we can rely on any divine intervention. I told Foy you'd just write a check out of your petty cash fund and that would end the matter." Vickers scowled.

"She's suing the network too?"

"And the production company, which you may remember, belongs to me, two ex-wives, and a bevy of children I have trouble keeping track of. The only person she hasn't filed against is the actress who played the part." Vickers sighed deeply. "But it's still early in the day."

"This is bullshit!" Larry shouted.

"Right. "Unfounded," "unwarranted," "without grounds," and "totally ridiculous." Those were the words of the large staff of expensive attorneys the network employs to ward off instances such as these."

"Then why do you look so damned worried?"

"Because, pal o' mine, the lawyers do not decide the case. They just defend. Some gray-haired old coot in black robes makes the final decision. This could set a very bad precedent. It could make the *Born Innocent* trial look like a small claims court."

"You can't sue somebody over a character portrayed on a TV show, for God's sake!"

"Why, because it's never happened before? Wise up, Larry. You can sue anybody for anything these days. Here. Look at this. Where is it?" He fumbled in a mess of papers on top of the file cabinet behind his desk. "Here it is, yesterday's paper. Some broad in Portland is suing her doctor for a hundred grand because she can't perform oral sex anymore." Larry looked incredulous as Vickers waved the newspaper under his nose. "She says the doctor left a piece of plastic tubing in her throat after an operation. She coughed it up three days later and she claims she has this fear of choking to death every time she gives her husband head." He pushed the paper hard into Larry's gut. "You want to tell me about suing again?"

Larry began pacing up and down in front of the desk. He was starting to feel nauseous. "This is absolutely insane."

Vickers opened a desk drawer and brought out a bottle of J & B he kept there for medicinal emergencies. Larry watched him pour a shot into a glass, waiting for Vickers to hand it to him. Instead the producer downed the drink himself and capped the bottle. "I'd offer you one, but somebody's got to be steady during this crisis."

Larry fell back into his chair. "What now?"

"Well, we got three choices. We can go to trial and prove you were mentally incompetent when you wrote that script and throw ourselves on the mercy of the court—"

"Get serious, will ya?"

Vickers raised one hand and began ticking off the options on his fingers. "Okay, one: We go to court and fight it. We prove you wrote a stereotyped character that is standard in most sales-oriented businesses. If we win,

169

and I emphasize *if,* it's going to cost us a bundle anyway, and the publicity isn't going to be good."

"Come on, Ned. You know as well as I do something like that'll boost the ratings four or five points overnight."

"Foy doesn't seem to give a shit about the ratings at this point, Larry."

"He must really be worried."

Vickers went on with his count. "Two: We settle out of court. Your wife's attorney has already indicated they wouldn't be averse to a fifty percent buy off."

"Great."

"And three: The one we all agreed we like the best. You go to your wife and get her to drop it. Bribe her, sleep with her, move back in, whatever it takes to get her to withdraw the action."

"I'll strangle her, that's what I'll do," Larry said angrily.

"That hadn't been one of the options we considered, but speaking personally, I'd go with that."

Larry got up and walked to the door. "I'll get back to you."

"Soon, fella. The hounds are barking up my pants leg and I can feel their hot breath on my balls."

SEVENTEEN

It was a miserable day. All was wrong with the world. Well, Larry theorized, as he walked down the long hall, it could be worse, it could be raining.

As he passed his office door Patte ran out and called after him. "Where you going?"

"Home. I've got some thinking to do."

"Wanna borrow my umbrella?"

Larry stopped and turned back to face her. "It's raining, right?"

"Actually, it's only a light drizzle. The heavy stuff keeps bouncing off the ozone layers."

Larry leaned against the corridor wall. "Some days, it doesn't even pay to be Italian," he mumbled.

"Huh?"

"I said, I've been giving serious thought to getting out of show biz and going into a more honorable profession like mugging."

"Is there a difference?"

He walked back to where she was standing and kissed her lightly on the lips. Taking her by the shoulders he held her at arm's length and stared into her face. "Whatever happens," he said dramatically, "I want to remember you like this—lovely, bright, and irreverent."

171

"You swear that on the Bible?"

"Hmmmm, the Bible," he said, doing his worst Groucho Marx impression. "saw the movie, must read the book. See you around, Gordon."

He walked away leaving Patte standing in the center of the hall. "Yeah, DiaMonte, see you around."

Larry drove around aimlessly, trying to line out the best course of action in his mind. First things first, he finally decided. He stopped at a phone booth and looked up the address of Cline's office. It was on Olympia near Western, and fifteen minutes later he was stomping into the posh anteroom, past the astonished girl at the reception desk, and into Cline's inner sanctum. The smaller man was sitting at his large oval desk in his shirt sleeves, talking into the phone.

Before he could look up at the grim specter that was advancing on him, Larry crossed the room and grabbed the receiver from his hand and slammed it into the cradle. "What the fuck did you mean by that crack about Lynn?"

Cline quickly wheeled his chair back out of reach of the madman that confronted him. "Have you flipped out?"

Larry went around the desk and took Cline's tie in his hand, lifting the little man to his feet. "Friend, I'm in no mood to be double-talked. What did you mean when you asked if I got my money's worth?"

Cline's close-set eyes bulged as Larry increased his grip on the tie. "You really don't know, do you?"

Larry pulled Cline's face close to his. "I'm not going to ask you again."

Cline sputtered for breath and nodded vigorously. Larry let go and pushed him back into the chair. As Larry towered over him like a crazed Goliath, Cline loosened his tie and tried to straighten the collar of his expensive

172

shirt. He began talking rapidly. "Jeeze, I'm sorry, Dia-Monte. I thought you knew, I really did. I didn't mean nothin' by it, I swear." Cline's Brooklyn twang was surfacing, a sudden alteration of his usual smooth diction. "She's a call girl."

Larry glared at Cline. "Don't shuck me, Raymond, or I'll feed you into that intercom box, and you'll come out on your secretary's desk a hell of a lot thinner than you already are."

"I wouldn't lie to you, Larry." It was "Larry" now. Maybe they were really long lost brothers. "She's—she's not exactly a call girl . . ."

"What would you say she exactly is, Ray? Little Miss Marker?

"Ah, she's a female escort. Only goes out with the real biggies. Word has it she gets better than a grand a date."

"*A thousand dollars?*" Larry's voice echoed in the paneled office.

"That's what I heard, Larry, just what I heard. I wouldn't know from personal experience. You gotta believe that."

"Nobody's worth a thousand fucking dollars a trick! Nobody!" On the other hand, he mused, he was the one who had written that check to Robyn.

"I swear, man, it's just what I heard around. I could be wrong. Yeah, that's it, I'm probably wrong." He looked up at Larry with a pitiful expression on his face. "You want me to be wrong?"

"Why should you be?" Larry remarked in defeat. "I seem to be the only one that's wrong today." He turned and walked out, leaving Cline sitting there shaking.

Larry was a very confused man as he drove home. He felt better for the confrontation with Cline. Who the fuck was he kidding? He felt like the last thing in the world he could

173

hang onto had just been taken away from him. And it was still raining.

He parked the car in the garage and entered through the kitchen. He stopped suddenly near the refrigerator and looked under the overhanging cupboards at the patio door in the living room. It was open, and rain was soaking the rug around the threshold. Shit, he never forgot to close and lock that door. He must really be losing his grip.

He walked into the living room and stopped with his mouth open. The entire corner wall was empty. His twenty-five inch Zenith Panorama, the component stereo system, and the big speakers were gone, along with the RCA video recorder and the rack of tapes. He moved to the dining room, afraid to look. The spot where his typewriter had rested on the stand was just a dusty square on the brown wood, and his desk lamp was missing. They stole his pewter-fucking-lamp, too!

He turned and ran up the stairs to check the top floor. Evidently they hadn't had time to do a thorough job or they could just carry so much. His gold chains and clothing were untouched.

He went back to the ground floor, called the police, then sat in the middle of the living room floor with a bottle of Scotch to await their arrival.

He didn't have to wait long. Within an hour, two uniformed officers showed up, poked around the jimmied patio door nodding a lot, then made out their report. Larry gave them the serial numbers of everything that had been taken, advising them that he had etched his driver's license number on all the hardware, something he now thanked God he had had the foresight to do after years of being lax about that sort of thing. It was some consolation, however minute.

The police left, after telling him the chances of recovering any of his property, even with the identifying marks, were about as good as taking the Rams and ten points in the Superbowl. He sat back down at his desk and swigged from the now half-empty bottle and stared at the vacant corner. "Dammit all to hell!" he shouted at the wall. This was all he needed to finish the day. He felt like packing a suitcase and heading for Crete. Fuck, the Cretins were probably in their monsoon season anyway.

He was getting angrier as he sat there. Then he noticed the carbon-steel carnation in the wicker basket on the corner of his desk. It was tilted at an odd angle. He got up and looked down into the basket. Then he started to laugh hysterically.

The steel stem rested in the small block of styrofoam he had used for a base. There was one lone penny in the bottom of the basket. The bastards had gotten away with what must have been thirty bucks' worth of pennies. That was okay though. He had engraved his social security number on each one of the coins. Now that was funny. He was still laughing as he carried the bottle to the sofa and fell on the cushions. All right, you asshole, he asked himself, are you going to sit here like a fucking patsy while the bird of fate defecates all over your face?

Yes, I am, said Larry.

No, you're not, said the Scotch.

I can't win, moaned Larry.

Who cares if you win or not? You're a Jewish fighter pilot, remember, commented the Scotch dryly.

"You're fucking right I am! Larry yelled at the ceiling.

He locked up the house as best he could and pounded on Lynn's door. Getting no response, he scribbled, "See me as soon as you get in," on a business card and stuck it in her mailbox.

He ground his teeth as he drove to Robyn's office, not even noticing half the signal lights. As he approached the low glass and brick building, he shifted down into second and laid a trail of rubber into the parking lot, sliding the nose of the Porsche up to the main window of her office. He glared out the windshield as he leaned on the horn, keeping it depressed for a full minute until she finally got up from her desk and came outside.

He could see Lee in the back of the office. The creep looked scared even though he followed Robyn out, hanging a few steps behind her. Larry got off the horn and stepped out of his car as Robyn came up. "If you're going to create a scene, Larry. I swear, I'll call the police."

Larry reached back into the Porsche and picked up the summons. Then he waved it under her nose. "Lady, I'm about to make the great quake look like a Sunday school picnic. What the hell is this all about?"

"I think you know damn well what it's all about." She was getting mad and her lower lip was beginning to tremble.

Lee was about four feet away and he looked nervous. "Anything I can do, Robyn?"

Larry spun on him, his fists balled at his sides. "Go back inside, Lee. Please," Robyn said without taking her eyes off her husband.

"Yeah," Larry said quietly, "before I step on your head."

He was looking for an excuse to bend Lee's face just a little and he hoped the other man would get brave. Instead, Lee just nodded and went back inside. He sat watching with one hand on the phone.

"I've had it, Rob, I really have. I'm not going to take anymore of your shit," Larry said, as he poked her in the chest with the summons.

"You slandered me and you're going to pay for it. Why don't you go shout at your lawyer instead of harassing me?"

"Shout? You haven't heard me shout yet!" Larry raised his voice about two hundred decibels. "You think I'm

176

going to take this crap lying down, you're round the bend, darlin'." His voice grew cold. "Drop it, babe. I'm warning you."

"Oh, you're going to threaten me now, huh?" She threw her shoulders back defiantly and stuck out her chin. "I can see the headlines now: Big Time Writer Hits Estranged Wife Because She Won't Sit Still While He Tries to Make Her Look like a Fool."

"Estranged is a good word for you, Rob. And nobody has to make you look like a fool. You succeed nicely at that all by yourself." He paused for breath. "You going to drop this bullshit or not?"

"Never happen."

"Okay." He went nose to nose with her, his eyes flashing angrily. "If that's the way you want it. I'll tell you this, and you better carve it in granite. I'm not going to settle. I don't give a big rat's ass if the network cancels the show or Vickers fires me. I'm going to court and admit I patterned that character after you. Then I'm going to prove that you really operate like that. I may lose the case, Mrs. Dia-Monte, but the resultant publicity is going to make Marvin vs. Marvin look like a scene from *Love Story*. I'm going to get up there on the stand and tell the world just what you are, and baby, I lived with you long enough to be able to prove it. It may cost me, but I'll see that you lose your license at the very least, bitch."

Robyn pulled back, trembling. "You do what you have to do."

Larry laughed. "You bet that tight ass of yours, lady. See you in court." Larry left her standing there in the middle of the parking lot as he drove off.

The phone was ringing when he got home. "You all right?" asked Patte, after he had grunted a harsh hello.

"Why is it that everybody's concerned about my welfare? Yeah, I'm just fine. Anything else?"

"Excuse me for living." *Click.*

Pretty soon he wouldn't have anyone left. The doorbell rang and he mulled over that thought as he opened the door to see Lynn standing there like a vision of bright sunlight. "Hi. Got your note. Sounded important."

He grabbed her arm and pulled her inside, slamming the door. Leading her to the sofa, he pushed her down hard. "How well do you know Ray Cline?" he asked her.

"What is this, a test for *Who's Who?*" She was still grinning.

"I asked you a question."

Lynn kept her composure. I've seen him around a couple of times, maybe at a party or something."

"What kind of party?"

"What the hell is this, Larry?" For the first time she looked around the barren room. "Where's your furniture?"

"I was robbed. What do you do for a living, Singer?"

"What?"

"You heard me. I speak very clearly, enunciating each word as I go. Try to read my lips. How do you earn your daily bread, your sustenance, your wherewithal? How do you pay your rent?"

She looked frightened for a moment, then shook her head. "We've been through that. What do you want to do, check my credit rating before you date me again?"

"You're a whore," Larry said softly.

Lynn stiffened. "What did you say?"

"You heard me."

She rose. "See you around, DiaMonte."

Larry pushed her back on the sofa, none too gently. "Answer me."

"Did you ask a question? It sounded more like a

universal condemnation."

"You know what I mean. You're a whore."

Lynn looked up at the ceiling. "My God, I haven't heard that word for years. I'm surprised you didn't say harlot."

"You sell your body. By any other name, it's the same thing."

Lynn inhaled deeply. "You sanctimonious son-of-a-bitch!" She glared at him like Robyn had, but somehow her anger was different, almost justified. "That's right! I sell my body. Same as you. Same as the rest of the world. You goddamned double-standard hypocrite!"

"You're a hooker," Larry said sadly.

Lynn jumped up and this time he didn't try to stop her. She pushed him in the chest with the palm of her hand like a kid screwing up nerve for a fight. "No, Mr. DiAMonte, I'm not a hooker. I'm not even a prostitute." He backed as she advanced on him. "I'm a female escort, and I get top dollar for what I do, just like you. I work two, maybe three nights a week, and I make a good living."

He was up against the wall now with no place else to go. "But I came up through the ranks, baby. After my husband and kids died, I tried to kill myself twice. I wasn't much good at that, so I just wallowed in my own self-pity for a long time. You know all about that, don't you?" She pushed on his chest again, and her head bobbed back and forth in anger. "Yeah, I was a hooker. In the beginning I did it all. From quick blow jobs in parked cars to nurse calls on seventy-year-old bastards that couldn't get it up for hours. You know what a nurse call is, fella?"

Larry winced. "No."

"Tell me something," she continued. "What about your TV starlets that go out with an agent or producer, go to dinner and a show, and end up in the sack to get one line in a commercial, or worse, a 'don't call us, we'll call you'?"

"That's different," Larry said defensively.

179

"Really? I'd call it prostitution. Dishonest prostitution at that. Well, buddy, I'm at least honest about what I do." She lowered her head and fought for breath. "Oh shit, I've seen your kind so damned many times before it makes me want to scream. Just leave me alone, will you?"

She was about to cry. Larry reached for her and she recovered and slammed his hand away. "Leave me alone, I said."

"Why did you get involved with me?"

She caught her breath and calmed a bit. "Because I found something genuinely nice about you. I was getting very close to you and I didn't want it to end. You know what? I haven't worked in two weeks. Want to hear how dumb I am? I was even thinking about chucking the whole business and falling in love with you." She shook her head and sighed. "I should have known better. You're just like all the rest."

"I was falling in love with you."

"Yeah, well, I'm sorry about that. Guess you'll just have to find yourself a nice virginal, simple and loving person."

"I don't go in for ten-year-olds."

"Is everything a joke to you, Larry? This isn't funny. We have what you call a relationship problem here. What are you planning to do now?" She looked up at him with moisture-filled eyes. "Pat me on the ass, forgive me, and try to reform me?"

"Make a hell of a story," Larry mused.

Lynn exploded. "You dirty bastard!" She clenched her fists and looked around for something to throw. Picking up a vase from the end table, she smashed it against the fireplace. It shattered to bits all over the hearth.

"That was a FedCo special," Larry said. "Two dollars and ninety-eight cents."

Lynn grabbed her purse and violently pulled a twenty dollar bill from inside, slamming it down on the coffee

180

table.

"I don't have change," Larry said.

Lynn screamed and tossed her head menacingly. Then she lifted a potted plant and sent it after the vase. The dirt and roots spread all over the carpeting.

Larry looked down at his fingers, folding them back one at a time. "You still got nine and a half dollars coming."

Lynn snarled at him and stomped for the door, slamming it so hard that a framed picture fell from the wall to the tile floor, breaking into several pieces and scattering glass everywhere.

Larry looked at the broken frame and shards of glass. "Now we're even."

EIGHTEEN

Larry drove to a small tavern on Sepulveda that he frequented occasionally when he felt like a drink on the way home from work. There were a few singles at the long bar, but it was early, and the small group of tables was empty. He found a corner table away from the bar. A pretty waitress in a low-cut red blouse and tight hip-huggers glided over as he sat down. "Hi, what can I get you tonight?"

"A 40-B," Larry said, and smiled widely. She laughed and he ordered J & B on the rocks. She returned with the drink on her tray and he handed her a twenty. "Thank you ma'am, and keep the change."

The girl eyed the bill carefully to make sure she wasn't being hustled. "But that's a twenty."

Larry waved her away. "Who cares? 'Tis only money, lass, and money is not required to buy one necessity of soul."

The girl gave him a big smile and departed. He lifted the drink to his lips and saw Patte Gordon come through the front door over the edge of the glass. "I'll be damned," he muttered as she looked around in the semidarkness, spotted him, and came over to the table. "What the hell you doin' here?" he asked as she sat down across from

182

him.

"I was on my way to your place and saw you driving down Roscoe. By the time I got turned around you were six blocks away. Don't you ever stop for lights?"

"Sit down, take a load off your feet," Larry said, ignoring the fact that she was already seated.

"Man, you're wasted."

"I know. The Soviets have attacked. Little bastards are all over town throwing up roadblocks. And they're clever. They dress like L.A. cops."

"Buy me a drink?" Patte asked.

"Hell yes!" He turned in his chair and backoned to the barmaid. "Innkeeper! Another flagon of ale for my friend."

Patte leaned across the table. "Are we?"

"Are we what?"

"Still friends?"

Larry took her hand and looked deep into her eyes. "What do you want to do, sing 'Auld Lang Syne'?" Then he looked down into his drink. "Anyway, I sure don't need no more enemies."

The waitress came up beside the table and smiled at Patte. "A Brass Monkey," Patte ordered, "and some peanuts." The waitress left and Patte addressed her ailing boss. "What's the problem now?"

Larry looked up in surprise. "You haven't heard about QB VII and a half?"

"The lawsuit? Yeah, it's all over the set." Larry told her about his meeting with Robyn, but he didn't mention the scene with Lynn.

"The last time I talked to you, you were in a very bad place."

Larry squinted over the rim of his glass. "Ah, a year, a century, how time flies when you're having rum."

"And you're really flying, aren't you?" Patte observed.

Larry assumed a W.C. Fields pose. "On a wing and a

prayer, m'dear, a wing and a prayer."

Patte took in his disheveled appearance. "You even look different."

Larry broke into a fast-talking carney soto voce. "You are seeing, for the first time in any ring, the one, the only, Super Larry!" He raised his glass. "Salud."

The waitress wiggled over and placed a drink in front of Patte. Larry winked at her. "Keep the change." She winked back and walked away.

Patte did a take, then said, "But you didn't give her anything."

Larry jerked his chair roughly around the table and leaned over as he whispered conspiratorially in her ear. "Shhhhh, don't want everybody to know I'm faster than a speeding locomotive."

"I think that's bullet."

Larry looked around the bar. "Where? How'd he get his mustang through the door?"

Patte laughed and put her arm around his shoulder. "Hey, let's get out of here before you start doing your impression of the Hulk."

"I was you, babe, I'd go find me a more suitable drinking companion. You hang around with ole DiaMonte long enough and you're bound to get corrupted."

Patte swirled her drink with the tip of one finger and met his gaze straight on. "Come on, I know a nice place, some wine, a little music and—" she smiled brightly— "and we can corrupt each other."

Larry stood and hoisted his drink at arm's length. "Oh God, that men should put an enemy into their mouths to steal away their brains."

"What the hell's that supposed to mean," Patte asked as she rose to steady him.

"It means, fair lady, so a little wine could hurt?"

On the way out Patte fished in Larry's pockets. "The

other side, Flash, I dress to the left," he commented as she came up with his car keys. "Hey, wait a damn minute, I can drive."

Patte stopped at the side of the Porsche and unlocked the passenger door. "How you going to drive and watch for the Red Air Force at the same time?"

Larry considered her logic for a moment. "You gotta point there," he said, as he collapsed into the passenger seat. When they were underway he tried to shift for her, but she kept pushing his hand out of the way. Finally he let it rest on the curve of her thigh. She made no attempt to remove it.

Patte screeched into a parking lot under a large neon sign that read: THE SADDLE HORN. "You're kidding," Larry said as she parked between a pickup camper and a new Corvette.

"You'll love it!" she beamed, as she dragged him from the car. The interior of the place was as big as a football field. One long wall was the bandstand, and what seemed to be hundreds of tables sprouted like weeds around a large dance floor. The entire place resembled a giant tack room, saddles and bridles decorated all the walls, and the bar looked like a corral. A very loud five-piece Western band was playing "The Queen of the Silver Dollar" as Patte pulled Larry into the mass of bodies on the dance floor. "See? What'd I tell you? Neat, huh?" she shouted over the noise.

"It's bedlam," Larry yelled back.

"Not right now, I thought we'd have a drink first," Patte deadpanned back as she led him across the dance floor to the tables. They sat at a vacant table on the periphery of the crowd. Larry said, "I can't hear you!"

"I didn't say anything."

"Fine, thank you, and yourself?"

The music built to a shattering crescendo, then ended

with wild applause from the dance floor and the tables. Larry clapped like a madman. "You really liked them, huh?" Patte asked.

"I'm applauding because they stopped. Jesus, how can you stand it?"

Patte smiled. "Like anything else, you acquire a taste." Larry made a face as a young girl in cowboy regalia and a white ten-gallon hat approached to take their order. Patte looked up and said, "One Tequila Sunrise, please."

Larry gave her a piercing look and said, "My good woman, I will have a vermouth cassis, French Vermouth, not Italian, and stirred, not shaken."

The girl shuffled her feet and shook her head. "I don't think we have those."

Larry pounded the table. "What? My God! How low have we sunk?"

The young cowgirl smiled sweetly and spoke between her teeth. "I don't want any trouble, buster."

Larry looked at Patte and winked. "Nor I, ma'am, for trouble troubles those who trouble trouble, right, Flash?" Patte nodded solemnly while the waitress shifted impatiently. "Okay," Larry relented. "Make it two Tijuana Nightmares then, what the hell."

As the waitress moved away the band broke into a slow, sad ballad. "Let's dance!" Patte grabbed his hand.

"To dance, my dear girl, one must first be able to stand."

Patte dragged him to his feet. "Come on, you can do it."

Once out on the floor with Patte's arms wrapped around his waist and her head nestled on his shoulder, Larry decided he could do it without falling down. It was easier than skating. "See, you're not so bad," Patte encouraged him.

Larry gave her a wide grin for her show of confidence, then tried an intricate step, bending her backwards with one hand around her waist and the other in the air. They both fell down.

Patte saved herself at the last second by scooting out from under his falling body, and Larry ended up with his nose in the sawdust, completely unscathed save for the large gash in his pride. Patte laughed and helped him to his feet and supported him as they staggered back to the table. Larry sat and finished his drink in one gulp, then gestured to the waitress for another round.

An hour later Larry had reached the point where a taxi could have run over his head and he would have tipped the driver. Patte was beginning to feel the effects of the liquor too, but it seemed she could match him drink for drink and still function nicely. "You know something?" she said with a slight slur. "You and I have never made love. Don't you think that's strange?"

Larry grinned like an idiot and rose. He began unbuckling his belt. "What are you doing?" Patte asked.

"Accommodating you."

Patte sat back with her hands behind her head and said nothing. Larry undid his belt and aimed the metal prong at her. "You know how to get a belt off?"

"No, but if you'll hum the first few bars, I'll try to pick it up."

Larry frowned and took the prong between two fingers and stroked it vigorously. Patte broke up and pounded the table with her fists. "Now that's funny!"

"S'okay," Larry said, as he sat back down. "I got a hundred of 'em."

"You mean a million."

"Nope, m'wife got custody of the rest." He laughed as he sipped his drink. The band was taking a break and it was relatively quiet.

Patte looked at him curiously and said, "I wanna go to bed with you."

187

"Now, now, now, Gordon, must keep the conversation clean. I am a married man." For some reason Larry found that extremely funny and he broke into a loud series of snorting chuckles.

"Then how about a sport fuck?"

Larry had a mouthful of booze and he almost spat it across the room as he fought to control himself. "Flash, you are crude, you know that?"

She narrowed her eyes and parted her lips. "You ain't seen nothin' yet, DiaMonte."

"The reason we have not found our way into each other's arms, sweet lady, is because I respect you. You're not like all the rest, you're regal. You belong in a castle somewhere with knights jousting for your favor."

"Shit."

"See what I mean?"

Patte came closer and pointed to man at a nearby table who was wearing a tan military-style shirt with red piping on the shoulders.

"See that guy?"

"Yeah?"

"Soviet infantry."

"But he's a blood."

Patte pointed a finger at Larry's nose. "Right. The lady at that table ordered a Black Russian."

Larry groaned, but Patte laughed enough for both of them. He watched her closely. When she laughed like that, her eyes sparkled and her little nose wrinkled up like an elf's. Maybe he'd reconsider her offer.

Suddenly he put his glass down and stood. "What's wrong?" Patte asked.

"Got to get some air."

They walked out together, her small body supporting his wavering form.

188

NINETEEN

Larry woke up very slowly. It was cold and he tried to pull the covers up around his head, but there were no covers. He opened his left eye halfway. The noise generated by the lid scraping the eyeball made him groan like a dying elephant. "Ohhhhh, God." He looked up and there was a mountain beside him. No, it wasn't a mountain, it was the side of the bed. He was lying on the floor, his face pressed into the shag of a cheap powder blue rug.

He struggled to a sitting position and noticed he was fully dressed except for one shoe. The room was a motel room, he was sure of that. He propped one arm on the bed and looked at Patte Gordon who was fast asleep, her hair fanned over the big pillow. The section of the bed next to her was rumpled. He must have rolled off during the night. The soreness in his bones told him it must have been early in the night.

Pulling himself up, he sat on the edge of the bed and held his head with both hands. "Oh shit." He looked around the floor for his other shoe, but it was nowhere in sight. "Hey," he whispered, as he nudged Patte. "You seen my other shoe?"

She rolled over on her side away from him and buried her face in the pillow. He could barely hear her muffled response. "I think you lost it when you kicked the watermelon down Sunset."

"Watermelon?"

"Maybe it was a casaba."

Larry staggered to the sink in the alcove off the bathroom and held his head under the faucet for several seconds. After he had toweled off, he searched his rumpled clothing for a cigarette. Finding nothing but a crumpled empty pack, he cursed and leaned over Patte. "Where'n the hell are we?" But she was in a deep sleep and even though he shook her, an act of violence that only served to increase the terminal ache in his left brain, she just mumbled and covered her head with the blanket.

He picked up the room key from the night stand. A bright pink piece of plastic attached to the key read: LA CASA MOTEL. He had never heard of it. No big deal; there were probably a dozen little hideaways like this that he hadn't scribbled in his address book. He walked to the door and pulled it open. His car was parked directly in front of the room. He looked up at a hazy gray sky. "Thank you, God."

It was colder outside. He could hear the sound of ocean breakers in the distance. Must be Santa Monica, he decided, but it sure was cold. An icy breeze whipped at his hair as he walked around the car, making sure it was all in one piece. Satisfied with his inspection, he found a cigarette machine in a hallway near the office and yanked a handful of coins out of his pocket.

There were five quarters, two dimes, several pennies, and a dead goldfish resting in the palm of his hand. He dropped the fish as if it were on fire, shook his head, and fed coins into the machine. Ripping open the pack, he walked to the edge of the parking lot to look at a road sign: WELCOME TO CAMBRIA.

Evidently it wasn't Santa Monica. But where the hell

was Cambria? Near Redondo Beach? He headed back to the room and sat on the side of the bed shivering. "Wake up, Flash."

"Let me alone to die in peace," was her forlorn reply. He shook her harder. "We're in Cambria."

"Great. Now shut up and let me go back to sleep."

"Just one question first."

"Make it quick."

"Where'n fuck is Cambria?"

Patte rubbed at the sleep in her eyes and sat up. The covers fell away exposing her breasts. "It's only a couple miles to the castle." She yawned.

Larry had a hard time keeping his eyes off her body. "What castle? I didn't even bring my passport. Which ocean is that out there?"

Patte looked at him in wonder. "You don't remember?"

"The last thing I remember is my twelfth birthday. God, my head hurts."

Patte got out of bed and padded to the sink and splashed water on her face. Larry studied her firm rear as she bent over, and then he let his eyes wander down the well-muscled calves to the tiny feet. "You don't recall propositioning the pygmy woman at the Safari Club in Oxnard?" Patte called from the sink.

"Pygmy woman?"

"Yeah, you told her you always wanted to meet a 'head' hunter."

Patte came back and jumped on the bed, sitting cross-legged and staring at him, completely comfortable with her nudity. More comfortable than Larry was. "Just before you went for a swim in the fishpond. You were using a swizzle stick for a harpoon and yelling, about 'A mountain put to sea.'"

"Yeah, I seem to have a vague impression of swimming under water for a long time. Will you please put something on?"

Patte smiled and tilted her head to one side. "That's not what you said last night."

Larry blushed. "Ah—did we—" He pointed to her, then to himself. "Did we—I mean—"

Patte laughed and reached for her Levi's on the floor next to the bed. "No, we didn't. I had to carry you in and put you to bed. You were in no condition to—"

"Right, I understand," Larry interrupted before she could embarrass him further. "So where are we?"

"Just down the road from Hearst Castle."

"What?"

"You wanted to take me to a castle, Sir Knight. That's exactly what we did. Why don't you take a shower and change so we can have a fun day."

"Change into what?"

"There's a suitcase in the trunk of your car. I didn't have the strength to lug it in last night. We stopped by your place and grabbed a few things before we left."

"For San Simeon?"

"Only castle in town, pal."

"But Vickers is going to have a coronary."

"So send him flowers," Patte said, as she pulled a sweater over her head. He was kind of sorry to see all that white skin disappear. "You grab the shower first," Patte said, as she headed for the door. "I want to run a couple miles, then I'll get the stuff out of the car." She opened the door and looked back. "We'll have a monster breakfast, then do the castle. You'll love it."

Larry gagged at the thought of food, and Patte laughed as she closed the door.

192

TWENTY

The waitress brought a giant platter of steak and eggs, hash browns, and rye toast, and set it in front of Patte. Larry stared down into his lone cup of black coffee. He was feeling somewhat better after a shower and a change of clothing. He was beginning to believe he might just live if he didn't have to stare at the human garbage disposal across from him.

Patte winked and stuffed a forkful of scrambled eggs into her mouth, following it with a quarter-slice of toast and chasing the whole horrible mess with orange juice. Larry shuddered and sipped at his coffee as the waitress came back carrying a plate of pancakes. Larry looked up. "Oh, Christ."

Patte grinned innocently at the matronly woman and swallowed. "We're on our honeymoon," she announced brightly.

"Oh, how nice. Congratulations." The waitress placed the plate beside the others. "Did you get married here?"

Patte said, "Yes," and Larry said, "No," simultaneously.

The waitress shook her head and walked off in confusion. Patte stabbed a piece of rare steak with her fork and waved it in his face. "Will you smile for once, Grumpy? This is the best thing that could happen to you.

You needed to get away from that rat race and lay back a little so you can get your head together."

"That's for sure." Larry rubbed at the back of his skull.

"Why don't you have something to eat? You'll feel better." She pushed the stack of pancakes under his nose. "Here."

"Because I don't want to offend your patrician sensibilities by throwing up all over the table."

Patte shrugged. "Suit yourself," and went back to eating. A pretty blue and white bird landed on the outside sill of the window near their table. Patte watched it as it pecked at the glass. "I used to have a canary named Spot," she said, as she pursed her lips at the bird.

"Creative name for a bird."

"Yeah, he was a real clown. Couldn't fly," she said, between mouthfuls. "Used to run across the rug and trip when he got his claws caught in the shag."

Larry flagged the waitress. "Miss, could you bring me a couple of aspirins and a glass of water? Thanks."

"I got a picture of Spot on my shoulder," Patte remarked, as the waitress left.

Larry leaned across the table and took her by the arm, turning her shoulder toward him. "Really?"

"No, dummy, not like that."

"What you mean, Flash, is that you have a photograph of yourself with your canary perched atop your shoulder, right?"

"Hey, you're beginning to wake up. Welcome to the club. You know what your trouble is, DiaMonte?"

"No, but I have the feeling you're going to tell me."

"You're uptight all the time. You never relax. Kick back like you did last night more often and all these minor problems that plague you will dissipate like the morning dew."

"Minor, huh?" Larry laughed.

194

"See! Already you look more human. Stick with me, and I'll have you back in your Dr. Jekyll suit in no time."

Larry reached over and picked up a pancake with his fingers, then stuffed the whole thing in his mouth. he furled his brow and chewed vigorously.

"Alllllllright!" Patte beamed.

A half-hour later she was dragging him away from the ticket booth across the pavilion toward the bus loading area at the base of the hill below the castle. It had warmed a bit and several dozen tourists lounged on the big yellow buses. It was a slow day and they had no trouble getting on a Tour One bus that was just about to leave. Patte handed the tickets to a young man in a blue uniform at the kiosk. "We're on our honeymoon," she said, as she pulled Larry close.

"No smokin' on the bus," the man said.

As they boarded, Larry said, "Either he's not a romantic, or his alimony is acting up."

They sat on the gray naugahyde seats and Patte immediately lowered her window to stare out at the low hills they were about to climb. The bus quickly filled with a group of camera-toting tourists and several noisy children.

Halfway up the winding road that led to the castle, Patte pointed out the window. "Look, there's a zebra!"

She's like a little kid, Larry thought, as he spoke over the running commentary the bus driver was reciting on the speaker. "I thought you had been here before?"

"I have, but I'm easily impressed. Why don't you lose that callous attitude and enjoy yourself?

"I'm thinking."

"I thought I smelled wood burning."

Larry held up three fingers close together. "Hey Flash?"

"Yeah?"

"Read between the lines, huh?"

Patte laughed. "Okay, I'm sorry. What were you so immersed in?"

Larry leaned over and whispered in her ear. "I was just wondering what it would take to hijack this place."

"The bus?"

"No, dummy, the castle. Picture if you will, a movie of the week about half a dozen guys that take the hill and hold the castle for ransom."

They were approaching the crest of the hill at the base of the castle. "Hey, yeah," Patte said with enthusiasm. "Say three guys on two buses. They stop them at the two roads and block off the top of the hill with the buses."

"And," Larry said animatedly, "they clear out everybody at gunpoint and dig in for the siege that they know will come." He gestured at the low terraces around the castle. "It's a perfect defensive position. You could hold it indefinitely."

Several other passengers were beginning to watch the two conspirators with expressions of concern. "Okay, comedy relief: the place is loaded with gold. We have one of the bad guys, a real schlep, try to bag some of the stuff and he's constantly concealing candleholders and the like on his person." Patte was caught up in the creation of the story line and her face glowed.

As they filed out of the bus she pointed to two Egyptian statues. "That's the goddess of evil, sickness and pestilence."

Larry smiled. "I can't get away from her, can I?"

Patte indicated the open terrace just above the black statue. "Two fifty-caliber machine guns set up there could command the entire low ground."

One of the tourists, a middle-aged woman with blue hair, was talking to a uniformed tour guide and nodding in their direction. The guide walked over. "Ah, excuse me, is everything all right?"

"I'm Dr. Gordon, the eminent psychologist, and this man is my patient. I'm trying to regress him to a previous life so I can cure him of his mad desire to imitate the sounds of hoofbeats by clapping coconut shells together."

The young man looked to Larry for help. "We're writers," Larry said, as if that would explain any deviant behavior. Evidently it was enough. The guide smiled and nodded, then walked to the head of the group and began his welcoming lecture. Larry took Patte by the shoulders and looked at her seriously. "You know, Flash, I think even on a hazy day you can see forever."

Her eyes clouded up and the smile left her lips. "That's the nicest thing you ever said to me. Let's go back to the motel."

"How can you think of sex at a time like this? A time when we're surrounded by such majestic opulence, such overpowering beauty. Why, the pages of history are unfolding before our very eyes. How can you entertain thoughts of carnal lust when confronted by this noble, imposing dignity?" he said, as he swept his arms in a large circle.

"Easy. I just visualize your big c—"

"Patte!" Larry shut her up by placing his hand over her mouth, then smiled weakly at all the turned heads.

The tour wound its way through the guest house and along the side of the massive outdoor pool. Larry gawked with the rest of the group, while Patte spiced up the guide's running spiel with little comments of her own. As they went through the Morning Room of the main house, Patte indicated a narrow stone staircase off to one side. "Come on, let's sneak upstairs."

"You're crazy," Larry whispered.

"They got some really ace bedrooms up there. We just

197

find one and lock the door. I took the Do Not Disturb sign from the motel."

Larry managed to quiet her as they entered the flag-draped dining room with its silver serving dishes and long wooden tables set with the camping china and the ever-present ketchup bottles. The tour ended at the indoor pool. The group stood on the inlaid tile that surrounded the deep blue water. Patte knelt and removed a nail file from her purse and began to pry at the strips of gold leaf between the dark tiles. "Want a souvenier?"

Larry grabbed her and hauled her to her feet before she could deface a state monument and land them both in jail. "You're bananas, you know that?"

"That's why you love me."

"I never told you I loved you."

She grinned slyly. "You will."

The sun was beginning to set by the time they got back to the car. They had dinner at the San Simeon restaurant: thick fillets and baked potatoes with all the trimmings. They both attacked the meal with vigor, sipping wine and cracking jokes about the day's antics. "That film we saw in the projection room," Larry said, as he chomped on a dinner roll.

"Ah, yes, Charlie Chaplin and Adolph Monjou. Seldom have I seen them looking so good. Musta been the altitude."

"I was thinking about Marion Davis."

"Shoulda guessed," Patte said, as she pushed her plate away. "Any particular reason?"

"With her hair a little longer and without that funny hat she could have been your twin sister."

"Oh wow, the family skeleton is finally out of the closet. All right, I admit it. I'm the illegitimate daughter of

William Randolph and Marion." She gestured at the salad bar. "Someday, all of this will be mine."

"I'm not kidding. The resemblance was astounding."

"You're just saying that 'cause you want to get me in bed."

"I don't want to get you in bed!" Larry said much too loud. He slunk down in the high-backed chair to avoid the curious stares from the other dinner patrons.

"I'll bet you say that to all the heiresses."

"Would you knock it off, Gordon?"

"Why?"

"Because you're embarrassing me."

"No, I mean why don't you want to get me in bed?"

Larry squirmed. He didn't have the answer to that one.

Patte stood. "If you don't agree to go back to that motel room and at least discuss the matter intelligently with me, I'm going to advise this entire roomful of people that I'm sixteen years old and you kidnapped me and have been committing sodomy on my person for the last two days."

"Waiter, check please," Larry sighed.

TWENTY-ONE

They entered the room and Larry headed straight for the bathroom. He undressed and hung his clothing on a hook behind the door. Then he showered, used the toilet, brushed his teeth, dried his hair and redressed. It had been a rough thirty-six hours and a part of him hoped Patte would be asleep if he stalled long enough.

She wasn't. She was fully dressed and sitting in a chair next to the small round table near the door. Her feet were propped up on the packed suitcase. The bed was made and Larry's down jacket rested on the chenille spread. He nodded at the suitcase. "What's that all about?"

"Well, the way you drive, I figure we can be back in town in a couple of hours. I get the distinct impression you'd be more comfortable that way."

Larry sat on the edge of the bed facing her. "Why the sudden change of heart?"

"Let's just say I'm a tease. This is the real me. I have this unscalable wall around me—"

"Bullshit," Larry interrupted her. "Did I all of a sudden become undesirable?"

"Noooooo, not at all. I just don't think you're ready for me yet. You know, you and I are good friends. Maybe best friends. Why fuck it up?"

Suddenly Larry found himself on the offensive. "Wait a minute now. I was all prepared to spend a fantastic night in the sack with you, and now you're coming on like a junior-high virgin."

"Boy, you could have fooled me."

"Look," Larry pleaded. "I don't think it's going to harm our friendship if we wrestle around in bed for one night."

"Maybe I'm looking for more than one night," was the soft reply.

"What are you looking for?"

Patte lowered her eyes. "Shit, I dunno."

Larry stood and took her by the shoulders, lifting her to her feet. He looked deep into her eyes and an expression of deep emotion crossed his features. "Patte?" he said with a catch in his voice.

"Yes?" she replied, as she raised a hand to caress his beard.

"You wanna fuck or what?"

She burst into a fit of laughter and pushed him back on the bed, falling on top of him. "You are crude, DiaMonte, you know that?"

He stroked her hair and kissed her. "I can be tender."

"Hmmmm, you want to show me?" She bit his ear, then licked it.

"Uh-uh, you first."

Patte disengaged and pulled the sweater over her head, throwing it across the room. She unzipped her jeans and stepped out of them. Larry reached for the light switch on the table lamp next to the bed, but she shook her head, looking at him through half-closed lids. "I like to see what I'm getting," she said honestly.

She wore no undergarments, and she perched on the edge of the bed as she removed her boots. Larry admired the curve of her back as she leaned down, the smooth

201

shoulders that were covered with freckles. Funny he hadn't noticed those before.

She stood back with her hands on her hips, her large nipples aimed right at his eyes. He rose quickly, kicked off his shoes and removed his shirt. Lowering his pants he stepped out of them, his erection straining against his Superman jockey shorts. His hands went to his sides to slip them over his hips, but Patte moved forward and knelt in front of him. "Let me do that."

Her head was opposite his groin and she inhaled deeply as she pulled the shorts down. His penis sprang out of the cloth and she took it gently in one hand. "Ohhhh, that's nice," she breathed as she kissed its tip then ran her tongue down the shaft to his scrotum. Larry stepped out of the shorts and pulled her up to his face, kissing her fiercely.

They clung together for a moment, his penis firm against her stomach, then she grabbed his shoulders and hoisted herself up so that he could enter her. "Ohhhh, my God!" she screamed, as he grasped her buttocks and pulled her tight to his chest. "Good, good, good." She moved up and down on his penis, her legs wrapped around his hips, her arms circling his neck in a death grip.

Larry's legs were against the bed and he sat down, then sprawled on his back with Patte sitting astride him. "Tell me what you like," she moaned, as she looked down into his eyes, an expression of total contentment on her face.

"I want it to be good for you too." Larry reached up and took her breasts in his hands, running the nipples between his fingers.

"Don't worry about me, lover. I came the second you entered me. It's your turn, so just relax."

Larry sighed and moved his lower torso in rhythm with her rolling thighs. She straightened up and raised her buttocks so that she could slide up and down the full length of his erection. Then she placed her left hand behind her and stroked his penis as it slid in and out of her. "Jesus!" Larry moaned, as he spread his legs wider to enjoy the full effect of her hand as she pushed him hard into her, then squeezed on the downstroke.

Larry reached for the dark patch of now soaked hair between her legs, but she brushed him away. "I'll do that, you just watch," she said, as she used her free hand to caress her clitoris and the top of his penis at the same time, while her other hand still held him from the rear.

He was getting close, and she could tell by the grunts and the arching of his back that it wouldn't be long. "No, Larry, not yet." She lifted her body from his and still holding his penis tightly, went to her side with her back toward him. Larry was surprised at her agility as she raised her left leg and moved down on him. He braced one knee under him so he could gain the traction necessary to pump into her and as he did, she groaned loudly. "Oh yes, I can really feel you like that."

He moved over her, spread her calves with his hands and slammed her buttocks with his thighs, trying to keep in time to the way she moved up and down. She turned her head slightly on the pillow and looked back at him, her delicate features intense. "I love the way you move me around, putting me where you want me. Your hands are so strong . . ." He grabbed her buttocks and squeezed hard. She raised higher as she began to climax again.

He drove into her as hard as he could. His whole body was on fire as the sound of his breathing became louder than her moans.

He came and he thought he would never stop. She reached back and grabbed his hips with both hands, holding him so he couldn't withdraw from her. "It's so beautiful," she gasped, then she started to cry. Huge sobs racked her body. Larry lifted her leg and swung her toward him until they were face to face, her tears soaking his chest.

"I'm sorry. Did I hurt you?" he asked with concern.

"No, I, ah, sometimes it's so good that I cry."

"You sure?"

She kissed his nose. "You're lucky, sometimes I laugh hysterically." She nibbled on his lower lip. "I love you, you stupid bastard. Do you know that?"

"I love you too, you dumb bitch," he said, smiling.

Patte scrunched in closer and pressed the full length of her body to his. "I hate to say it," she hesitated.

"But?"

"I told you so."

TWENTY-TWO

The sun set over the Los Angeles basin. Larry DiaMonte unpacked his suitcase, tossed it in the bottom of the bedroom closet, and went downstairs. He spent a half-hour rearranging his furniture to cover the large bare spot left by the burglary, then made himself a tuna fish on white. He took the sandwich and a beer into the living room, turned the radio he had brought down from the bedroom to an FM station, and settled back to enjoy his dinner.

He had taken Patte home earlier that afternoon as soon as they pulled in from San Simeon. She had asked him when she would see him again, but he had been vague. He knew she felt the coolness in his voice, but he made no effort to explain his feelings. Hell, he wasn't even sure what they were himself. They had had a fantastic night together; that he would testify to under oath. She was a great woman: tough, tender, intelligent and soft, very soft. Maybe it was just him. Maybe he couldn't love anybody anymore.

He was lighting a cigarette when the phone rang. "Have you had dinner yet?" the soft female voice asked.

"Who is this?" Larry grumbled, not recognizing the voice.

205

"Beth."

"Who?"

"Bethany Drew. You know, kinda tall, marginally good-looking, the one that hangs out with Kent Jacobs," she said sarcastically.

"Oh, I'm sorry, Beth." Larry snubbed out his cigarette in the desk ashtray and sat down, pencil poised over a scratch pad. "What can I do for you?"

"Well, have you?"

"Have I what?"

"Jesus, for a writer you have a retainability factor that's amazing. Have you had dinner yet, Mr. DiaMonte?"

"Ah, no, why?" Larry lied.

"Well, Kent just called from Atlanta and he won't be coming in for another few days. Something about buying a football team, I think. He suggested I get together with you and go over some points in the script. Purely for my benefit, he's not concerned, but I'd like to clarify a few things. Are you busy?"

"Hell no."

"Good. Why don't you come over and I'll fix us something to eat. Won't be fancy; all the help's gone because I wasn't expected back myself till tomorrow. I'd invite you to bring Lynn along, but I'm afraid it's going to be mostly work."

"Ah look, I wouldn't want to put you to any trouble. We could go out somewhere."

Bethany laughed. "Please, I don't think I could stand the stares today. Come on, it's no trouble."

See you in an hour." Larry hung up and downed the remainder of his beer.

Bethany Drew opened the door and smiled. She was wearing a yellow silk kaftan, her normally fluffy hair

206

bunned to the back of her head. She wore no makeup—or a great deal. Larry couldn't be sure. She could have just stepped out of the shower or Sassoon's. "Hi."

"Good evening, Ms. Drew. I was in the neighborhood and saw the searchlight beams."

"Too bad you didn't get here earlier. We take the barrage balloons down at sunset. Come on in."

She led him down the long hallway that seemed to run forever. They pushed through the swinging doors into the kitchen. Larry hadn't been in the kitchen before. It was big enough to land a Cessna in, with room left over for a couple of Greyhound buses. Copper pots hung everywhere from heavy wood beams that ran the length of the room. A large open-hearth fireplace took up one wall and several free-standing chopping blocks were scattered near a bank of ovens.

Bethany motioned him to a huge antique table that had probably been used by the Plymouth colony on the first Thanksgiving. She went to one of four refrigerators set in an alcove. "I hope you don't mind cold food. I was too beat to make anything fancy."

Larry squirmed into one of the high-backed chairs at the table. "No, that's fine."

She came back to the table carrying a silver tray piled high with pastrami and bagels. Larry swallowed hard and grinned. "Ah, my favorite."

Bethany pulled over a stand that bore an ice bucket and poured wine into pewter goblets. Lifting hers in a toast, she said, "Here's to *Bonnie and Clyde Revisited*."

Larry looked confused. "Why that?"

"That's what we decided to retitle the film. Figured it would have a built-in audience."

"You're kidding."

Bethany laughed. "Of course I'm kidding. Are you all right?"

"I'm sorry. I had what we call in the trade a bad week. You'll have to excuse me if I'm not up to my usual sharp repartee."

Bethany daintily spread cream cheese on a piece of pastrami with a small silver knife, then stuffed it in her mouth. "Wanna tell me about it?" She smacked her lips as she watched him thoughtfully.

"Why?"

"Because you look like you could use a friendly ear right about now."

"Are you and Kent happily married?" Larry blurted out without thinking.

"Is that a proposition, Mr. DiaMonte?" Bethany replied coyly.

Larry flushed bright crimson. "Hell no! I—I just wondered—"

Bethany licked a bit of cream cheese from one finger and got up. "I'll be right back." She returned in less than a minute carrying a large leather portfolio. Pushing the tray out of the way, she set it down and opened it. "This, my good man, is the only reason I asked you over here tonight." The portfolio held a stack of pencil sketches, the top drawing being one of Bethany in her usual model's pose.

Larry looked at it carefully. "You want to find out if I can pull some strings and get you into television?"

"Flip it over, writer."

Larry did. The next sketch was one of a black man in a naval watch cap and peacoat. No, it wasn't a man, Larry realized, as he leaned in for a better look. It was Bethany. He went to the next one quickly; Drew made up as a toothless ninety-year-old woman, then another with her as a middle-aged bald man. "Who did these?" Larry exclaimed in wonder.

"Ron Garetson."

"Christ!" Garetson was one of the top makeup people in the business. He had gained his reputation from a rash of science fiction films five years ago and ever since he had been in great demand for anything that required the odd or unusual.

"Well, what do you think?" Bethany prodded.

"I'm flabbergasted. Can he really make you look like that?"

"He says he can. I believe him. Question is, do you?"

"Why is my opinion so important?"

Bethany sighed. "Because I want to know if this is the way you envisioned the script. I mean, after the switch from male to female lead."

"It's—it's fantastic," Larry said in awe, as he thumbed through the sketches again. "But what the hell do I know? I backed Austria in World War I."

Bethany took his arm and looked straight into his eyes. "I've got to go into this thing full bore, Larry," she said seriously. "Kent is convinced I can do it, but I'm not as certain as he is. I need to know what you think, what you really think."

Larry sat back and took a drink of wine. "Frankly?"

"No, I want you to lie to me! Shit, yes! You wrote the script; if anybody should have a handle on it, it's you. I need an objective opinion. All I hear from Kent and Frankel is, 'Sure, baby, no sweat, a piece of cake, you'll blow their doors off, kid.'" She paused for breath. "I'm still the one that has the final say, 'cause I'm the one that's got to stick my ass out there for everybody to look at."

"You want the truth?"

"Yes," she said softly.

Larry smiled. "I think you'll blow their doors off, kid."

"Really?" She brightened.

"I wasn't sure before, but if you're that concerned about doing this thing right, I'm in your corner. Anything

209

you want from me, you just ask."

Bethany came to her feet and kissed him on the cheek. "Thank you, sir. I appreciate that. You've really helped me make up my mind."

Larry closed the portfolio. "Anybody else seen these?"

"Hell no. I told Ron if he so much as breathed a word about it, I'd personally castrate him with one of his dull inking pens. He'll keep quiet, but he knows the whole concept."

"What?"

"Well, hell, he's the only one that can do it, so I figured I better level with him up front. I considered telling him that I just wanted the pictures as a gag, but he's sharp as hell. Anyway, I wanted to get his creative juices flowing, and now he's as excited about it as you and me."

Larry's respect for Bethany had been on the upswing ever since he sat down at the table. She was a real pro. He winced at that thought.

She caught the look of pain on his face and took his hand. "Come on." She grabbed her goblet and the wine bottle and led him out of the kitchen.

"Where we going?" Larry asked in alarm.

"You just come with me and shut up."

She led him into the library, pushed him down on the sofa, and refilled his wine cup. Then she sat on the thick rug at his feet and said, "All right, if I'm going to work with you on this film, I want to know what the hell's bothering you. I want the whole story from the beginning, so you better start talking or you'll never get out of here."

Larry made himself comfortable on the cushions and began to talk. He spoke for almost an hour, telling her about Robyn, Lynn and Patte. He left out nothing, going over the lawsuit in detail, his confrontation with Lynn, and his mixed emotions about Flash. For some reason it felt good to discuss his troubles with a relative stranger. It was

210

almost cathartic.

Bethany listened intently without interrupting. When he was finished, she said, "Jesus fucking Christ."

"Hopeless, huh?"

"I'll give you seventy thousand for a renewable six-month option, on the condition I get to play the part of Lynn."

"It does sound like I made it up, doesn't it?"

"Didn't you?"

"I wish I had," Larry sighed.

Bethany took another sip of her wine and looked up at him. "Want some expensive advice?"

"Is there any other kind?"

"Nope. Go talk to Robyn. Try apologizing for making her look like a fool. I know that's going to be a new approach for you, but it might work. I don't believe she's the total bitch you make her out to be."

Larry shook his head and looked at her like she was a candidate for the retard ranch. "What good could that possibly do?"

"Let me ask you one first. Why did you two split up?"

"Shit, I dunno. She fell in love with somebody else, I guess."

"You sure that's the reason? Maybe you drove her to somebody else."

"How?"

"Hey, I'm no marriage counselor! But I can think of a dozen ways. Did you beat her? Did you take her to bed often enough? Did you fool around?"

"No, definitely, and only in my heart."

"Very funny. That may be part of your problem. You're a funny guy, Larry. Sometimes being serious is good too." Bethany waited for a response that didn't come. Larry just stared down at the carpet. "If you married her in the first place and lived with her all those years, she can't be all that bad. There must be some compassion in her some-where. Try and look for it. If you look hard enough, you might find a way to communicate. That's my advice. What the hell do you have to lose?"

"God, you're a dreamer, Drew, you know that?"

"Goes with the territory, DiaMonte." She rose and took his hand. "Go home and think about it. I've got to get some sleep. Early day tomorrow." She walked him to the door and they hugged.

"Hey."

"Yeah?" she said.

"Thanks for the pastrami, huh?"

"Anytime, pal."

Larry drove home. As he turned the corner into his street, he saw the green Seville parked in his driveway.

TWENTY-THREE

Larry parked in the street and walked to the side of the Caddy. Robyn was leaning against the headrest, staring straight ahead at the garage door with her window down. He studied her profile for a moment before he spoke. "If you're waiting for the light to change . . ."

She turned and looked at him. "Hello, Larry."

"How long have you been here?"

"Not long. I'd like to talk to you." It was dark and he couldn't tell by her expression what she was planning this time, but he was sure it would do her justice. He opened her door, controlling his smile very carefully.

"Come on in and I'll buy you a drink."

Once inside, Robyn stood in the center of the living room looking around while Larry mixed drinks at the bar. He watched her from under lowered lids as he stirred the drinks. Walking over, he handed her a glass. "You can sit down if you want."

"Thank you." She sat on the edge of the sofa, as if she was ready to bolt at the slightest provocation. She looked uncomfortable but resigned. When Robyn looked resigned, Larry knew it was time to head for the bunkers.

"To better behavior," he said, as he raised his glass. She nodded and sipped her drink. It must have taken a lot of courage for her to come to his home, Larry decided as he watched her. If there was to be another confrontation, she'd be at a definite disadvantage on his turf. It must be something serious. "The kids okay?" he asked suddenly.

"They're fine. Steve had a science project, growing plants in a closed environment or something. He tilled the soil under the house and set up Gro-Lights near the crawl space in the hall. Paid for them with his own money." She spoke quietly, without looking at him. "He said they were nasturtiums."

"I always said the kid was creative."

"The plants turned out to be marijuana."

"Oh Christ!" Larry paled.

"I think you better have a talk with him."

"Yeah, yeah, I will . . . but you have to admit he's got chutzpah."

"That's not the main reason I'm here. I—" She was interrupted by the sound of the door bell.

Larry got up and went to the door, wondering who the hell it could be at this hour. It was Patte Gordon. "You going to stand there with your mouth open, or you going to invite me in?"

"Ah, sure, come in."

Larry closed the door behind her as she stepped down into the living room. "Hello, Rob." Patte nodded at Robyn.

"Hello, Patte." Robyn didn't attempt any further conversation and Patte looked to Larry for help.

"Ah, we're just having a little talk, is all." He spread his hands and shrugged.

"Then I won't intrude. I just wanted to pass a bit of information on to you, but I guess you already know."

"What the hell are you talking about, Flash?" Larry asked.

"I'll tell him," Robyn said. Patte nodded and headed for the door.

"Now wait a damn minute . . ." Larry followed her. Patte opened the door just as Lynn was reaching for the bell.

Oh fuck! Larry almost shouted as Lynn brushed past Patte into the entry hall. "I left my earrings," she said menacingly as she swept by Larry to the living room. She snatched up the silver earrings off the end table next to Robyn, who stood at her approach.

"I'm Robyn DiaMonte," she said, extending her hand to Lynn.

Lynn stopped and looked at her closely. "In that case, lady, you have my deepest sympathy." She turned abruptly, leaving Robyn with her hand extended, and headed for the front door.

Larry made a grab for her arm as she went by. "Lynn—"

She knocked his hand aside. "Out of my way, Boy Scout, before I deck you."

Patte leaned against the entry hall wall with a smile on her lips. Larry glanced at her. She winked. He could imagine what was going through that twisted mind of hers. He managed to get hold of Lynn again as he spoke to Patte. "I thought you were leaving."

Patte folded her arms across her chest. "I wouldn't miss this for an upstairs tour of the castle."

Lynn made for the door, dragging Larry almost off his feet. "Wait a minute. I want to talk to you," he begged.

She spun on him like a cyclone. "You can't afford it." Then she was gone. Larry watched her run down the walkway, then looked at Patte.

"Goodnight, Gordon. Don't let the door hit you in the ass."

"Damn, I always get sent out of the room when the fun starts."

Larry took her arm and set her outside on the stoop, closing the door behind them both. "What did you want to tell me?" he whispered.

"I got a new recipe for a morning after drink. One part cranberry juice, one part hot water, and a shot of semen. Tastes terrible, but you sure have fun mixing it."

Larry groaned and reopened the door. "Bye, Flash," and he closed the door in her face.

He went back to the sofa, sat next to Robyn, and gulped his drink. "Sorry about the interruptions."

"You have more traffic going through here than the L.A. Expressway." Robyn's eyes narrowed. "Who was the stunning one?"

"My next door neighbor."

"That's convenient." There was a touch of jealousy in her voice.

Larry ignored the reference to his sex life and charged forward boldly. "What was Gordon talking about? What is it you both know that I don't?"

Robyn relaxed back on the sofa. "I called my attorneys this afternoon and instructed them to drop the suit."

Larry almost fell off the couch. "You *what?*"

"You heard me."

"I heard you, but I didn't believe you."

"Would you like it in writing?"

Larry was astonished. "Why, f'chrisakes?"

"Because I think you would really make it a nasty, horrible battle. I've given it a lot of thought and decided I can't put the kids through something like that."

Robyn the martyr. "You were the one that started the whole business. Didn't you think about the kids then?"

"I didn't start it, but you're right, I just wanted to get even with you." She lowered her eyes and studied the glass in her hand. "If I were a better mother, I would have considered the children's feelings sooner. At least I'm grateful to you for pointing that out to me."

Robyn the saint. Was she really sincere, or was she just

216

trying to put him off his guard again? "So you're just going to drop the whole thing?" Larry snapped his fingers. "Just like that?"

"I already have. I wanted to explain it to you in person." She looked over at him, and he could see a trace of the old Robyn in her eyes. "Evidently I don't despise you as much as you despise me."

Oh oh. Robyn the contrite. That was the worst sign. Now's the time to throw her out, pal. Before she socks it to you again. "I don't despise you, Rob. I just don't understand you. I really don't know what the hell happened between us, and it galls me."

Robyn put her drink down on the table and took a cigarette from her purse. Larry let her light it herself this time. She surprised him by offering him one and holding out the lighter for him. Something told him to beware of estranged wives being cordial, but he puffed and nodded a thanks. She snapped the lighter shut, and he looked at her hands as she held it tightly. They were trembling. Not much, but enough to make him feel a little more in control of the situation.

"You want to know why we're not together anymore?"

"You're damn right I do."

"May I have another drink please?"

Larry got up and took her glass. By the time he returned from the bar she was composed. "I could never understand how you handle rejection like you do."

"What?" He handed her the glass and sat down.

"Remember last year when you were pounding on doors all over town trying to peddle the *Two Families* précis?"

"Like it was yesterday." Larry nodded.

"You used to come home and bitch about the stupid producers and ignorant story editors till I couldn't stand it anymore. But you never gave up. It was always the next

217

one that would buy it, or the one after that. You were so damned confident, so sure of yourself and your talent. You remember the day Lear kicked you out of his office?"

"Yep."

"I was rejected seventy-two times that day."

"But who's counting, right?" Larry said lightly.

"I was. I couldn't handle it the way you did. I knew I was good, but I got scared every once in a while. I'd find myself driving to a listing appointment or an open house, and I'd burst into tears for no reason. I was very unhappy, Larry."

"Then why didn't you say something?"

"I did. You just never heard me. So I lived with it eating at my insides, while you made a joke of every serious situation that came along. You're not a bad man, Larry. You just never grew up."

"And you're a senior citizen, huh?" Larry asked sarcastically.

"That's not wrong, Larry. It just wasn't right for me. I tried to live with that, God knows how hard I tried. I wanted to understand you, and I hoped that someday you'd change. When you started abusing the kids, I couldn't take it anymore."

"What? Oh, that's a good one, child abuse now! When you reach, babe, your arms are ten feet long. I haven't raised a hand to either of those two in years."

Robyn's eyes were beginning to moisten. "You abused them mentally. You were always the strict disciplinarian. You never complimented them on their accomplishments, you just grunted and drove them like you drove yourself. You expected them to be as good as you were, and when they failed, whether it was L.J. not being able to hit a ball or Steve getting a C in English, you never sympathized. You just censured them for not trying harder." She was crying openly now. "Steve used to ask me why you didn't love him." She stared at him with a stream

218

of tears on each cheek. "How could I answer him? What do you say to your son when he asks why his father doesn't love him?"

"You are good, you know that? You are really marvelous. Why don't you just admit you fell for somebody else and dumped me instead of doing this bullshit number on me about the kids?"

"I didn't begin a relationship with Lee until after we separated. I needed somebody who was more like me. Somebody who could understand me. Somebody who wasn't as cocksure of themselves as you were." She paused and wiped at her eyes. "It's very important to me that you believe that."

God, he wanted to believe it. More than anything, he wanted to believe it. "You lying bitch! You've been fucking him for over a year behind my back! You wouldn't know honesty or fidelity if it smacked you in the face!"

Robyn rose and opened her purse, removing a long white envelope. "I didn't think you'd believe me. But I had to say it anyway." She placed the envelope carefully on the coffee table. "Please don't open that until after I've gone."

"What is it?" Larry growled.

"It's the last tie, honey. The last piece of pain." She walked to the door. Larry made no effort to restrain her. He stared at the envelope a long time after she left, thinking about what she had said. Finally he reached over and picked it up, weighing it in his hand. Then he ripped it open.

It contained a check made out to him. A check for four thousand dollars.

TWENTY-FOUR

Larry didn't go into the office the next day. Instead, he drove to Venice and sat on the sand, watching the surf break against the beach. It was sunny and warm. He watched the young lovers snuggling on blankets and an old couple wading in the shallow waters.

Just before noon a movie company moved out on the sand near a big rock outcropping. He studied them as they laid down furniture pads to set up their cameras. The extras huddled around, maneuvering for position when the cameras rolled, like hawks swooping from every direction to get in the shot, acing out their comrades at every opportunity. Most of them were just kids, hardly much older than Steve.

He thought a lot about Steve. Nasturtiums, huh? The kid sure had guts. He'd have to have a talk with him. A long talk.

When he got home he picked the newspaper off the stoop and went inside. There were thirteen messages on his answering machine. He keyed the first one. "This is Gordon. Look at the vital statistics section of today's *Trib*. Tallyho."

He unfolded the paper and opened it to the vitals. He scanned the column headed "Final Decrees" with his finger, then he began to laugh hysterically. He was almost doubled up as he ran to his car with the page in his hand. All the way to Robyn's office other drivers looked at him as if he were a madman.

He swung the Porsche into the parking lot and leaned on the horn, still contorted with laughter. Robyn ran out and came up to the side of the car. "Are you nuts?" she screamed. Same old Robyn.

He just handed her the paper and pointed to the line. Robyn squinted at it: "Final Decrees, DiaMonte, Robert, Lawrence."

Larry managed to catch his breath and sputter. "I always said you had balls, but now my opinion has been borne out by the *Los Angeles Tribune*."

Robyn began to laugh. "Who sues them, you or me?"

"Now that's funny," they said in unison and then they broke up. Larry staggered out of the car and leaned on Robyn for support. Robyn sat on the fender and held on to his arm to keep him from falling down.

When they both were calm again, Larry looked at her and said, "You know, I really did love you."

"I know. I loved you too."

"Maybe next time around, huh?" Larry grinned.

Robyn smiled sadly. "I think I've used up all my lives."

"No way." He kissed her. "See you around, DiaMonte."

"You too, DiaMonte."

He got back in the car and started the engine. She leaned on the driver's door. "Where you bound for now?"

"There's a lady I have to apologize to. I hope I haven't waited too long."

"Which one?" Robyn really was curious.

"I'm not quite sure yet." He waved and pulled out.

On the way back home he fumbled in his shirt for a cigarette and came up with an empty pack. He shook his head and pulled into the parking lot of the first liquor store he encountered.

As he came out of the store opening a fresh pack, he looked at his car. A red Jensen Interceptor was backing out of an adjacent parking slot and heading right for his Porsche. "Hey!" he yelled. "Watch it!" But his warning came too late. The Jensen smacked his car with a dull thud and crumpled the driver's door like wet paper. "Son of a bitch!" He ran to his mangled car as the other driver got out of the Jensen. "Don't you ever watch where you're backing, you stupid—"

The driver of the other car stood there looking destroyed. "I'm sorry," she said. "I didn't see your car. It was all my fault, really. My insurance company will take care of all the damage."

Larry looked at his broken car, then back at the woman. She was the most beautiful lady he had ever seen. "Ah, it's nothing, just a scratch, don't worry about it. My name's Larry DiaMonte. I write movies."

She smiled at him. A 36-D. It was going to be a fantastic day.

NICCHIA
Geoffrey Wagner

Price: $2.75 0-505-51782-5 (cc: 50)
Category: Historical Romance

Nicchia was young, beautiful and married to a powerful Italian nobleman. When Italy fell into the hands of the Austro-Hungarian empire, the count believed that he would do well to send his lovely wife as an envoy to enlist Napoleon's help in regaining his country. If anyone could gain the Emperor's sympathy, it would be the tempting Nicchia. But the count's plan to save his country took an unexpected turn, and the diplomatic mission blazed into a fiery romance between Nicchia and the most powerful man in the world.

SEND TO: **TOWER BOOKS**
P.O. Box 511, Murry Hill Station
New York, N.Y. 10156-0511

PLEASE SEND ME THE FOLLOWING TITLES:

Quantity	Book Number	Price

**IN THE EVENT THAT WE ARE OUT OF STOCK
ON ANY OF YOUR SELECTIONS, PLEASE LIST
ALTERNATE TITLES BELOW:**

Postage/Handling
I enclose .....

FOR U.S. ORDERS, add 75¢ for the first book and 25¢ for each additional book to cover cost of postage and handling. Buy five or more copies and we will pay for shipping. Sorry, no. C.O.D.'s.

FOR ORDERS SENT OUTSIDE THE U.S.A., add $1.00 for the first book and 50¢ for each additional book. PAY BY foreign draft or money order drawn on a U.S. bank, payable in U.S. ($) dollars.

☐ Please send me a free catalog.

NAME_____
(Please print)

ADDRESS _____

CITY _____STATE _____ZIP_____
Allow Four Weeks for Delivery